TDY

TDY

Douglas Valentine

Clarity Press, Inc.

© 2020 Douglas Valentine

ISBN: 978-1-949762-20-4
EBOOK ISBN: 978-1-949762-21-1

In-house Editor: Diana G. Collier
Cover Design: R. Jordan Santos

ALL RIGHTS RESERVED: Except for purposes of review, this book may not be copied, or stored in any information retrieval system, in whole or in part, without permission in writing from the publishers.

Originally published by the author in 2000 via Authors Choice Press, an imprint of iUniverse.com, Inc.

Clarity Press, Inc.
2625 Piedmont Rd. NE, Ste. 56
Atlanta, GA. 30324 , USA
http://www.claritypress.com

To my loving wife Alice

But that I am forbid
To tell the secrets of my prison house,
I could a tale unfold whose lightest word
Would harrow up thy soul, freeze thy young blood,
Make thy two eyes, like stars, start from their spheres,
Thy knotted and combined locks to part,
And each particular hair to stand on end,
Like quills on the fretful portenpine:
But this eternal blazon must not be
To ears of flesh and blood.

Hamlet
Act 1, Scene V
William Shakespeare

Introduction

After I was discharged from the Air Force in 1970, I enrolled at Fulton-Montgomery College in New York, and in the fall of 1971 I transferred to the Rochester Institute of Technology. The incidents I am about to relate happened at Fulton in the spring of 1971 and at Rochester in the fall of 1971. These incidents had to do with the fact that I was a member of the Vietnam Veterans Against the War (VVAW).

Please allow me to explain.

I had joined the VVAW in early 1970 while serving in South Vietnam as an English language instructor in an obscure Air Force program known as Operation Palace Dog. I'll tell you more about Palace Dog later on, but for now it's enough to know that I had come to the conclusion that we, the Vietnam veterans, were being exploited by our government, and that the American public was being deceived by it too. So I turned against the war.

As you can well imagine, the VVAW in Vietnam was an underground organization composed almost entirely of enlisted men, most of whom occupied various rear echelon positions in personnel, or finance, or in a few cases as journalists with The Stars & Stripes. Some very important VVAW members were actually employed inside MACV headquarters in sensitive intelligence jobs that gave them access to the unvarnished and often unpleasant truth, as opposed to the overly optimistic propaganda that was routinely presented in official communiqués.

Being in the VVAW in Vietnam was considered subversive, and precariously close to treason, so I did not become an active member until I returned to the United States and started college. But then I did my part. When asked by the leadership to form a chapter at Fulton in order to educate the public about the realities of the Vietnam War, I did so without hesitation. And when I was invited to appear on a local TV show to testify about my own experience, I readily agreed.

I was living at my parent's house at the time, when a person at VVAW national headquarters contacted me and told me that Jane Fonda was planning to visit Fulton to speak against the war. Like most veterans we weren't happy that Ms. Fonda had allowed herself to be photographed while sitting and giggling on a North Vietnamese anti-aircraft gun in Hanoi. That was not our way of doing business, but the VVAW leadership wanted to capitalize on the publicity the sexy starlet would generate, and they persuaded her to become one of our sponsors.

The strategy worked. A local CBS affiliate in Schenectady learned that Fonda was coming to Fulton, and when she told them she wanted to work with the VVAW, CBS asked us to put together a discussion panel. It was their idea, but we liked it and we went along. A prominent VVAW leader came up from New York and stayed at my house, and when Fonda arrived at the airport we picked her up. I took photographs of her for the college newspaper, and for the VVAW, and we spent some time with her that evening while she met with the President of the Student Association.

The following day Fonda spoke to the student body at about ten o'clock in the morning, and later that afternoon we had our veterans panel discussion in a lounge in the Student Union building. There were five of us on the panel, all members of VVAW, each with a different story to tell.

They sat us at a cafeteria table in front of a bunch of microphones and TV cameras, and what with all the reporters, lights, and on-lookers, I was pretty nervous. In fact I was too nervous to listen to anyone else, and I really do not remember what any of the other veterans said. I do remember that I was the second person to speak, and that we each had ten minutes to tell our own individual story, and that I gave the ten minute version of the story that appears in the following chapters. I also remember that people in the audience were truly amazed at what I said. I didn't have time to go into detail, obviously, but my story was so bizarre and so different from what the other veterans had to say, that it just grabbed everyone's attention.

The CBS affiliate in Schenectady broadcast the show that night on local TV and I watched it with my parents at home. It was exciting, at first. They showed excerpts from Jane Fonda's speech before the energized student body, and they showed excerpts from our VVAW discussion panel, which was held later that afternoon. The only problem was, they omitted my story. As I later learned, CBS headquarters in New York had decided it was too controversial and had censored their compliant affiliate.

That was in the early spring of 1971, and in the fall I transferred to the Rochester Institute of Technology. Although disillusioned by my experience with CBS, and determined to spend less time on politics and more time concentrating on my studies, I agreed to set up a VVAW chapter at RIT. I held a few meetings, most of which were rather disorganized and uninspiring. I would bring in buttons and anti-war literature, and about ten people, some veterans, some not, would show up.

By then the Vietnam War was winding down and, as I mentioned, the meetings did not generate a lot of interest. But the VVAW was still at the top of the government's enemies list, and I remember that a couple of fellows claiming to be pro-military veterans attended the last meeting and complained that we were hurting the war effort. I don't know if it's true, but I had the feeling they were infiltrators sent by the FBI or military intelligence.

Despite the hecklers I gave my usual talk, the same ten minute anecdote CBS had censored, and that's when the trouble started. After that meeting I was approached by two men while I was walking to my car. It was cold and dark outside, and we were the only people in the parking lot. The man in charge was wearing a nicely tailored overcoat and a gray suit. He was about thirty years old with a crew cut and a pockmarked face, and dead eyes that made him look like a shark. The other man was wearing a navy blue pea coat and had the dull look of an off-duty cop. But the guy in the suit was definitely CIA; he presented his government credentials and said, "You've been talking too much about Laos. We don't like the words you're saying. None of it's true and if you keep telling lies, bad things could happen."

It was dark and they had come at me from behind, taking me by surprise, and to say the least it was frightening to know that the CIA was following me. I had just gotten married and when I told my wife she became terrified. We started to worry that our phone was tapped, and that the government would cut-off my financial aid. All of which, in view of my work with the VVAW, led to a general paranoia that in turn exhumed all the bad memories I had buried in my subconscious. I started having nightmares and flashbacks, and for the sake of my marriage and sanity I dropped out of the VVAW and entered psychological counseling.

To this day, more than thirty years later, I still feel threatened. I still have a lack of trust in the government. But my family is grown and for reasons that any Vietnam veteran will understand, I have decided that now is the time to come out of my shell.

I just hope the effort proves worthwhile.

Chapter One

Like a lot of young people growing up in the early Sixties, I considered myself something of a non-conformist—a person destined to follow his own star rather than the tired conventions of middle-class society. Romance and adventure were what I desired, as opposed to the nine-to-five rut my parents were stuck in, so I enrolled in a liberal arts college, intent on becoming a freelance photographer and world traveler.

Little did I know.

Reality quickly reared its ugly head and my irresponsible behavior landed me in academic trouble, and by the autumn of 1965 I found myself faced with the choice of flunking out or dropping out of college. It was not a difficult decision to make. Rather than flunk out and get drafted into the Army, I dropped out and enlisted in the Air Force, which had a much better reputation. And I did so without any reservations. I suppose it was a result of my strict upbringing, but claiming to be a conscientious objector or running off to Canada were alternatives that never entered my mind.

Like many people growing up in the Sixties, I was more conservative by nature than I pretended to be.

After my basic training I was assigned to an airbase in New Mexico and I moved into a comfortable two-story airman's barracks that resembled a lower-middle income housing project. My roommates were two well-connected airmen working in the base Personnel Office. The weather was hot and dry, the tempo slow, and the security extremely tight because there were nuclear weapons stored on our base.

The week I arrived I was put to work on the base newspaper. My main job was covering public affairs stories for the Information Officer, an affable, middle-aged major who took an instant liking to me. I guess he was impressed by my photography, which he said had very good quality and composition, and in a relatively short period of time he assumed the role of my mentor and surrogate father. Consequently whenever an enviable assignment came along—one involving travel away from our desolate base, as well as the company of VIPs—it was usually placed on my desk.

For example, I was assigned to photograph and write an article about Chappy James, the first black man to become an Air Force General. And for several months in a row I did articles featuring the base's "airman of the month", one of whom I photographed in the Houston Astrodome with Sandy Koufax and Don Drysdale, the dynamic pitching duo of the Los Angeles Dodgers. But my all-time favorite assignment was when I was ordered to Nellis Air Force Base in Nevada to interview Chuck Yeager, who was still the hottest test pilot in the world. The man was really great to work with, not like a lot of celebrities who let fame go to their heads.

Despite my brief flings with excitement, life on base was monotonous and boring. For entertainment we bachelors did one of three things: we comforted the lonely wives of Air Force officers on overseas tours; we drove to El Paso and crossed into Juarez where we enjoyed the Acapulco Gold, tequila, and cheap sex; or we traveled overseas on TDY (temporary duty) missions.

Of the three, TDY missions were the most appealing because they meant extra money as well as the opportunity to escape the tedious regimens of an isolated airbase. I personally knew airmen who traveled TDY to Vietnam to repair F-4 Phantom jets, and I knew a fellow photojournalist who had gone there to write articles on the airmen who were repairing the planes. Everyone who went to Vietnam returned with fantastic tales of easy women, inexpensive consumer goods like televisions and radios, and limitless opportunities to exploit the Vietnamese economy, which was raging out of control due to the massive influx of American dollars and servicemen.

Actively promoted and glamorized by the Air Force, TDY assignments were in great demand. But it didn't take too long before I got one. Because my roommates were employed in Personnel, and thus had a preview of all upcoming TDY assignments, my name was soon at the top of the sign-up list of people eligible for overseas duty. This "volunteer" list was periodically forwarded to the Human Resource managers at the US Air Force Military Personnel Center, where a screening board considered each applicant against the various requests coming down from the twelve separate Air Force Commands. It was only a matter of time until an assignment for a photojournalist materialized, and when it did arrive in the spring of 1967, it came as no big surprise that it was given to me.

It was a Monday morning. I had reported to the Public Information Office as usual and was sitting at my desk when the phone rang. It was the Personnel Director himself (not one of his junior officers, which is normally the case) calling to ask if I could come to his office immediately to discuss my request for an overseas assignment. The Personnel Office wasn't far from ours and it took about ten minutes to sign out and walk over.

A short chubby man, the Personnel Director got right to the point. "The overseas assignment you requested has become available," he said curtly and somewhat irritably, "but it won't be handled through normal channels."

I realized right away what the problem was; the Personnel Director was not being fully informed, and he didn't like it. Ordinarily the Personnel Director knows everything about everyone's comings and goings, and even the base commander knows only what the Personnel Director tells him about personnel matters. But my assignment, for some unexplained reason, had been taken out of his hands, and he found that hard to accept.

Looking at me with disapproval, as if I were to blame, he said, "But if you're still interested, we would like you to meet with the Base Security Chief, who will go into the matter in further detail."

I quickly agreed, my curiosity piqued at the prospect of being involved in some sort of special operation.

"Good," the pudgy man replied. "I'll make the necessary arrangements and you'll be notified when they're completed."

With that I returned to my office and, red tape being the rule, immersed myself in my work, not expecting to receive a call for several days. But to my surprise I got another call at the end of the day, again from the Personnel Director, notifying me that I had an appointment the next morning at eight hundred hours sharp with the Base Security Chief.

The mission hadn't even started yet, and already it was taking some unexpected twists and turns.

*   *   *

The Security Police on any airbase have two primary responsibilities. The first is to protect the base from outside attack. In war zones like Vietnam this task was handled either by the Army or the Marines, until 1969, when the Air Force developed its own airbase Security Teams. The second responsibility was for Public Safety—things like law enforcement, escort services for visiting dignitaries, the use of informants to detect pilfering and drug abuse, and the confinement of prisoners. It was a very important job and on airbases like ours, where nuclear weapons were stored, the Security Chief carried a lot of clout.

Considering the prominent function it performed, Security Police headquarters was located at the main gate—which meant I had to borrow a jeep and drive for ten minutes to get there. And when I got there the Security Chief did not disappoint me. He was everything a cop should be, and more. Tall and husky with muscular arms and a square jutting jaw, he had just returned from a tour in Vietnam and had packed his office with memorabilia, including an AK-47 (technically illegal to import into the United States), a Viet Cong battle flag with streamers, and photos of himself with various South Vietnamese and American honchos in and around Tan Son Nhut Airbase outside Saigon. The most prominently displayed photo was of our Security Chief with Premier Nguyen Cao Ky, the swashbuckling and excessively enterprising commander of the South Vietnamese Air Forces.

The Security Chief, evidently, was very well connected and very gung-ho.

After dispensing with the usual formalities, he told me that his superiors had briefed him about the up-coming assignment, and that he was to act as my liaison with the "using agency." Having spent nearly a year in the Air Force by then, I assumed he meant either the National Security Agency (NSA) or the Defense Intelligence Agency (DIA), both of which occasionally borrowed Air Force personnel and materiel. What was especially intriguing, however, was his hush-hush approach. Although not required to do so, he took great pains to explain that he was the only person on base with even the slightest idea of what the assignment entailed.

I was duly impressed and the Security Chief proceeded to say that, in his opinion, I was well suited for the job, which would involve a brief period of familiarization and proficiency training to be conducted at another base in preparation for a "photo-recon" mission outside the US. He did not foresee any danger, but aside from the usual overseas pay, I would receive hazardous duty pay and a substantial bonus upon completion of the task. The whole process of training, traveling, doing the job, and returning was estimated to take about thirty days. The mission was classified Top Secret, however, and therefore I would *not* be kept informed about the details. More importantly, I was strictly forbidden from discussing the mission with anyone—not even to say I was on it.

At this point the Security Chief asked me, "Do you have any questions?"

Affecting my finest military persona—standing a little straighter and aiming my eyes just above his—and trying not to appear too mercenary, I replied, "Yes, sir," and asked how much the pay and bonus would amount to.

The Security Chief ran down the pay scale, and when he said the bonus was twenty-five hundred dollars, I nearly lost my breath. Twenty-five hundred dollars was as much as I earned in an entire year.

"Are there any other questions?" he inquired.

There were none at the moment. I was still too stunned.

"In that case," he said, "think it over for a few minutes and if you're still interested (did I detect a note of sarcasm), we can put you in touch with the people in charge of this thing. And if they're satisfied, they'll cut your TDY orders and arrange for your training right away."

Twenty-five hundred dollars was an awful lot of money in 1967, enough to buy a car, and the dollar signs were flashing before my eyes. But I didn't want to appear over-anxious, so I pretended to mull the decision over for about three seconds, then I said, "I'd be very interested, sir."

The Security Chief nodded perfunctorily. "That's what we wanted to hear. You can expect to receive further orders in a day or two. Meanwhile, resume your normal duties and remember, you are not to discuss this matter with anyone. Understood?"

It was, and I was dismissed. Feeling elated, I drove back to the Information Office and dove into my work, trying hard not to act overjoyed. Not thinking about the mission and the money was the only way I knew not to mention the bonanza to my friends, which I was itching to do. However, as I look back on the situation, I realize the self-censorship also meant that I did not question why it was such a big bonus, nor did I ask myself why, if there really was no risk, there was hazardous duty pay. The whole thing was weird, but my philosophy at the time readily embraced weirdness. As the Merry Pranksters used to say: "You're either on the bus or off the bus." And I was definitely on it.

In any event, I didn't get much time to dwell on the subject. Once again the administrative machinery moved faster than anticipated and I was contacted the very same afternoon, right after lunch, by our upbeat Security Chief. He told me there was a "hop" leaving first thing the next morning for Eglin Air Force Base in Florida, and that "they" wanted me on it. Was that a problem? Could I pack an overnight bag and be ready in time? Knowing my friend, the Information Officer, would relieve me on a moment's notice, I said I definitely could.

"Good," came the curt reply. "Then it's settled. Your name will be on the flight manifest. Report to me when you get back. Good-bye, and good luck."

Chapter Two

A "hop" is any plane, big or small (but usually a C-123 or C-130), that travels nonstop from one airbase to another, moving personnel and materiel. Hops are the Air Force's version of public transportation, and there were frequent hops between all the major airbases on a daily basis, especially those, like ours, that were in the Strategic or Tactical Air Commands. Unscheduled hops were not uncommon either, enabling anyone with enough influence to move anywhere in the world on a moment's notice.

What was extraordinary about the C-123 hop I took to Eglin Air Force Base, however, was that I was the only passenger on it.

Eglin Air Force Base occupies a wide stretch of territory in the Florida Panhandle near Fort Walton Beach. It was my first visit there, but by reputation I knew it was the headquarters of the Special Air Warfare Center, through which all Combat and Forward Air Controllers passed on their way to Southeast Asia. As specifically stated in TAC Regulation 23-12, Paragraph 1, the mission of the Special Air Warfare Center is "to organize, equip and train assigned or attached personnel to participate in Special Air Warfare operations anywhere in the world," and "to conduct improvement in organization, equipment, doctrine and concepts of employment of joint land-air-sea forces in unconventional warfare."

When translated into layman's terms, all of the above means that Eglin was, and is, a very heavy place.

The instant I stepped off the C-123, I was stopped by a Security Policeman who checked my ID, put me in his jeep and drove me to the Security Police headquarters at Hurlburt Field. I was escorted to a numberless briefing room with nothing inside it except a table and two chairs. The guard stood at attention outside the door and a few minutes later a large man dressed in civilian clothes entered the room. He introduced himself as having field grade rank, but neglected to produce identification or mention his name. These were not oversights.

The man in mufti was formidable, at least six feet two inches tall and well over two hundred pounds, with an ache of toughness that befit a big city chief of detectives. He settled his bulk into a chair, cast an intimidating stare in my direction, motioned for me to be seated, and then stated that he was there to screen and prepare me for the assignment. In his hands was my personnel file.

For lack of imagination I'll call him Mr. Hammer, after Mike Hammer, the famous fictional detective.

Mr. Hammer began the interview with questions about my background, just to make sure I was the person I claimed to be. He asked for my father's name and my mother's maiden name, and their dates and places of birth. He asked if I had any brothers or sisters, and he asked for their dates of birth. And when he was finished with that, he noted that I had graduated top in my basic training class in hand-to-hand combat and armaments. That seemed to please him.

When he had established to his satisfaction that I was who I claimed to be, he told me that I had been selected for two reasons: first, because I was judged to be an excellent photographer (I was always a better photographer than journalist); and second, because I already had a security clearance, which conveniently absolved "them" from having to expend the time and energy of conducting a typical, extensive background check. He then explained that my instructions would come piecemeal as the mission progressed, and that, in the meantime, he would tell me generally what it was about, and specifically how I was to conduct myself.

To wit: upon receiving my final clearances I was to return to Eglin wearing my fifteen-o-fives (the standard Air Force summer weight uniform, consisting of a short sleeve shirt and pants), and that apart from an overnight bag I was *not* to bring along any personal effects. In addition, I was to remove my nametag and any other identifying insignia from my uniform. My military ID would be confiscated upon my return, at which point I would be introduced to the other members of the team, with whom I would receive special training in the latest and most sophisticated camera equipment the US military had to offer, in preparation for a Top Secret Photo/Reconnaissance mission in the Philippines. There was to be no fraternization with the other technicians, nor was there to be any discussion about our personal or military backgrounds: to do so would be considered a serious breach of security and would result in my immediate dismissal from the mission. If I did not already have a nickname, he suggested I invent one.

Then he paused and said very seriously, "The success of the mission depends upon your conducting yourself in accordance with these instructions. Do you think you can handle it?"

The swiftness of my sincere, "Yes, sir," surprised even me.

Hammer folded his beefy arms across his barrel check, eyed me warily for a moment, and then nodded his head ever so slightly. I knew right then I'd gotten the job.

In conclusion, Hammer said the team would remain in isolation once we were assembled, and that we would stay in isolation until the job was done. After our training we would fly to another airbase in the US, and then to Clark Air Force Base in the Philippines. We were to be thoroughly outfitted before our departure and although he did not foresee any danger,

I would receive hazardous duty pay and a sizable bonus upon successful completion of the assignment. I was aware of that, correct?

Indeed I was.

He relaxed and asked if I had any questions.

I did. "How many people will be on the team?"

"It'll be a small team," he replied ambiguously. "Ten, maybe twelve people."

"How many photographers?"

Tensing a bit at the directness of my question, he said, "A few."

"What will we be photographing, sir?"

"You'll be receiving that *specific* information later on, at the proper time," he replied curtly, "as I've *already* explained."

A person doesn't become a journalist without a knack for pushing people to their limit, so very respectfully I asked: "Sir, can you tell me about the type of training we'll be receiving?"

From the way he bridled, I knew that Hammer did not like being pumped for information. He was accustomed to asking the questions and his patience was wearing thin. But he gave in. "You'll be introduced to custom designed camera equipment and trained in its use. Details of this aspect will be presented to you during your instruction." Leaning forward, he grumbled, "Now, if you have no more questions...."

"No, sir," I said submissively, even though I had twenty questions I wanted to ask. But I didn't. Once again I suppressed myself.

"Fine," he said. "Your escort will take you back to the airfield and you'll return to your base. A final decision regarding your qualifications will be processed as soon as possible, at which time you'll be notified. You know how to conduct yourself. You're dismissed."

I was taken back to my plane feeling confidant that I would get the job, mostly because "they" seemed so pressed for time. My only disappointment was that the mission was in the Philippines, not Vietnam. But even if it wasn't going to be as exciting as I had hoped, the money and travel were still there, and if I did my job well, who knows, it might lead to bigger and better things? There was always that chance.

Again I chose not to dwell on the uncertainties. Back at the base that night I focused instead on what I could buy with twenty-five hundred dollars. An enlarger was a distinct possibility. A nice new stereo rated high, as did a fat down payment on a Ford Mustang. I was like a kid dreaming up a Christmas list. As I fell asleep, visions of sugarplums danced in my head.

*   *   *

My final clearances and TDY orders came two days later on a Friday, not from the Personnel Director, but directly from the hard-charging Security Chief. I got a call at my office saying he wished to speak to me in his office, "ASAP." And what he had to say was, "You've got the assignment if you want it."

I said I definitely wanted it.

"Then here are your orders," he said. "Take a good look at them."

On his desk was a standard TDY form; a single sheet of paper titled Temporary Duty Order—Military. At a glance it looked perfectly legitimate. The Security Chief had signed his name as the Orders Issuing Official, and the Personnel Director had signed his as the Orders Authenticating Official. The Purpose of TDY was Photo/Reconnaissance, just as I'd been told. The Itinerary listed a California APO Zip Code as my point of departure, and Clark Air Force Base as my destination. No problem. Approximate Number of Days indicated thirty, and all the biographical data was accurate.

I couldn't see anything wrong with it. Not that I expected to, or knew what type of irregularities to look for anyway.

"Have you seen your orders?" the Security Chief asked rhetorically.

"Yes, sir," I replied, showing no concern. But something about his detached manner put my journalistic instincts on alert. So just to be on the safe side, I asked, "Do I get a copy, sir?"

"No you do not," he snorted. "You've seen your orders and that's enough." Stiffening slightly and looking at me askance, he said, gratuitously, "You still want the job, don't you?"

I said I did. Even if I did have my reservations, I wasn't about to back away from twenty-five hundred dollars because of a single piece of paper.

"Good," he said, slipping the TDY order form in his top drawer. "Now that we've gotten that taken care of, you'll return to Eglin for your preparation. You'll be leaving tomorrow. Can you do that?"

I said I could.

The Security Chief was satisfied. "You know what to pack and how to conduct yourself?"

I said I did, and that was that. The next day I was on another hop to Eglin with only the foggiest notion of why. But that's standard procedure in the military. People come and go and no one asks questions, especially of superior officers. It's all part of the motivational indoctrination. When your job is done you go back to doing whatever you did before. You might unwind with someone you were trained with and live with, and trust implicitly. But you never talked to strangers. It was the same unwritten rule that applied to smoking pot on base: you simply did not put your business on the street.

As my sad little story will illustrate, this obsession with deniability was one of the nastier by-products of the Vietnam/Watergate era. Naturally the CIA started the practice and perfected it in the name of National Security. One of their people would hook up with a line outfit or a recon outfit; he would *not* be wearing a nametag and his name was either Smith or Jones. But the innocuous Mr. Smith always had the authority to tell everyone else what to do. Everyone resented it, of course, because trouble invariably followed on Mr. Smith's heels. But everyone eventually got used to it.

Eventually the obsession with deniability spread throughout the military, to the point where it became normal to assign ordinary people like myself to special operations. Our identities were meaningless. If a guy had a nose like a beak and bobbed his head, his name was Birdy. Places were equally irrelevant. All the hills and villages in Southeast Asia looked alike, and after awhile it was just too much trouble to keep track of where you were. Officers would never think it necessary to tell lowly enlisted men where they were on any particular day, and no one really cared as long as they got out alive. Place names only mattered if the action was heavy, or if a friend got killed.

Truth be told, this absurd emphasis on secrecy had to do with the fact that we were fighting a counter-insurgency in Vietnam. Sometimes it's called unconventional warfare, other times psychological warfare; but whatever you call it, it lends itself to secrecy because it's fought among civilians. Which means that a lot of innocent people get killed. Which is why secrecy is so damn important. For only by concealing its mistakes, its wrongdoing, and its outright evil deeds, can the government convince the people that God truly is on their side.

Chapter Three

The three Air Force Security Policemen waiting for me at Eglin wasted no time relieving me of my military ID, social security card, driver's license, and whatever else had my name on it.

No longer possessing documentary evidence of my existence—in other words, having been rendered a total non-entity—I was driven to a special operations facility on the outskirts of the airbase and then ushered into a building containing transient quarters large enough to accommodate an entire company of men. However, apart from my escort and me, the only people in the building were two heavily armed Blue Berets. The guards were stationed at a desk in the lobby, and I was led passed them down a corridor to a windowless room with two single beds, two dressers, a closet, and a table and a chair. The first person to arrive, I unpacked the little I had and scratched my head.

Three more people arrived over the course of the next forty-five minutes, each one arriving on a different plane from a different airbase, location never specified. Two were photographers and one was a soundman.

The second person to arrive was a tall, thin, lanky kid, no older than nineteen or twenty, with reddish hair and a Mid-Western accent. He was told to share the room with me and after the guards were gone, he introduced himself as Rusty, which was probably his real nickname.

I introduced myself as Pete.

We shook hands and Rusty began chattering about whatever crossed his mind. He wished he had a radio, for example, because there was a basketball game he wanted to listen to. Incidentally, what was my favorite team?

I explained that boxing and wrestling were my sports, and that I had little interest in football, baseball, or basketball.

"Hey, that's interesting," he said, bouncing to the next subject—girls. And on and on he rambled about nothing in particular, like he had arrived at summer camp. But I got the impression that Rusty was more than merely ingenuous. He seemed insecure and apprehensive. He never complained, however, and his lack of pretenses endeared him to me and right away I trusted him. I may have felt a little protective too, like an older brother. I imagined his ambition was to become a photographer for *Sports Illustrated*. Rusty seemed like that kind of guy.

While Rusty and I were unpacking the other two people arrived. The first was a stocky Mexican American with dark hair and rugged features. He was escorted to the room directly across the hall, and after the guards had departed, Rusty and I wandered over. Giving us a polite smile, he extended his hand and said, self-mockingly, "Everyone from south of the border is José, right?"

As we shook hands and introduced ourselves, I noticed he had a tattoo on his upper arm, just below the sleeve. It was a homemade tattoo of a cross with three dots, one above the top of the cross, and one above each of the branches. I think it indicated that he had been a member of a Chicano street gang.

Reticent and ready to obey the rules, José was not somebody to trifle with. He said he was there as our soundman, and after that he remained pleasant but aloof. Apart from the fact that he didn't want to make waves, he had the physically intimidating movements and mannerisms of someone who knew how to use his fists. I imagined that he was in the military for the training that would someday enable him to get a job in a Latino recording studio.

The fourth member of our team was escorted into José's room while Rusty and I were standing there. Well built and projecting an abundance of energy, he had curly blond hair and a fair but sunburned complexion. The hippie movement was starting to blossom, and after he introduced himself as Taurus, I got the impression he was heading in that direction; you know, toward San Francisco, to wear flowers in his hair.

* * *

I wish I could tell you more about Rusty, José, and Taurus. I wish I could fully develop their characters, and entertain and enlighten you with snippets of our repartee. But we never had any clever conversations, and after our initial introduction we stood there looking at each other, not knowing what to say. I remember that Taurus, in a feeble attempt to break the ice, made a stupid joke which Rusty, of course, picked up on. But José was not amused by their indiscretion, and he muttered something in Spanish—something that sounded like a cross between a curse and a prayer. He knew that Rusty and I had come perilously close to breaking the rules simply by wandering over to his room and introducing ourselves. And in fact, just as Taurus and José started unpacking their bags, the guards came by and told Rusty and me to return to our room and wait for further instructions.

The rules were *that* restrictive, and, truth be told, the four of us never spent any meaningful time together socializing as a group.

On the other hand we were still basically kids, even José. We were relatively naïve in the ways of the world, anti-authoritarian and defiant by nature, and had yet to become aware of the real reasons for our enforced isolation. We were being manipulated, yes, but we didn't really care; so the strict prohibition against fraternizing, at this early stage of its development, seemed ridiculous rather than sinister, and we connected in the unspoken, subversive sort of way that disobedient boys connect when they're sent to the detention hall for discipline. At times there was a snickering sense of trying not to laugh when the principal wasn't looking.

No one ever mentioned it, but there also was an unspoken bond of mutual respect that came from knowing that each of us, for some special reason, had been selected for this secret mission. That unspoken bond of respect grew as we saw how adept each one of us was at his appointed task. We knew we would work well together as a team—and given the chance, we might have enjoyed getting to know one another.

But we never got the chance. Big Brother dictated that secrecy, not camaraderie, was the key to our mission's success.

*   *   *

A few minutes after we had settled in the guards came to our rooms and escorted us, en masse, to a dreary, windowless classroom on the same floor of the building. The classroom was furnished with overhead fluorescent lights, a blackboard, and a large collapsible table with several chairs behind it, and a few more chairs lined up in front of it. They were the kind of chairs with armrests for taking notes. We were told to be seated and wait, and five minutes later the man who was to be our commanding officer entered the room. He was dressed in plain green fatigues with no unit insignia or sign of rank, and no nametag.

Dutifully we stood and saluted.

"Be seated," he said in a firm voice accustomed to giving commands. "I'm in charge of this project, and I'm a field grade officer, and that's all you need to know about me. But for the sake of convenience you can address me as Major."

He gave us the once over, noting our individual reactions.

"As you know," he continued, "we're going on a mission together, so I expect you to cooperate with one another. But," and here he set the tone of the mission, once and for all, "I do *not* expect you to be friends with one another. In fact, I don't even want you *talking* to one another, unless it's absolutely necessary. Is that clear?"

The guards had obviously told the Major about our little reception party, and the four of us responded with prompt and earnest yessirs to his stern admonition.

"Good," he said, having made his point. "You four people are here as our technicians, as our photographers and soundman. As you've already been told, we will be flying to the Philippines, and from there we will embark on a photo-recon mission into an area that will remain unspecified until we reach it. There will be additional briefings as we proceed, so control your curiosity and refrain from asking questions prematurely."

He paused for a moment and then continued. "You'll be utilizing some very advanced equipment, so before we launch the mission you will undergo an intensive training program. That's the first item on the agenda."

At that point the Major began outlining the training format and while he did so, I examined him closely. My initial impression, which later proved correct, was of a career commando. A Robert Conrad look-alike, the Major was of average height and weight, but heavily muscled, with dark hair in a crew cut, and a deep tan from spending a lot of time outdoors in hot places. He was about thirty years old, but an ugly scar across the bridge of his nose, extending under his right eye, and a reflective glint of Le Guignon in his dark brown eyes, combined to make him look older. You knew he'd spent his season in hell.

Raw physical power emanated from the man. A fitness fanatic, he was the type of soldier who did fifty push-ups (on his fingertips) and one hundred sit-ups (within two minutes) and ran five miles (fast) every day before breakfast. As he spoke in short clipped sentences, repeating the little we already knew, he projected an aura of consummate self-confidence that bordered on hubris. Apart from his high-energy level, that swaggering bravado was his most distinguishing characteristic. From the beginning of the mission there was never any doubt about his ability to command, coordinate, and direct our effort to its successful completion. Although unapproachable, he inspired trust.

During the fifteen minutes that he initially briefed us, the Major never indicated specifically what our advanced equipment would be used for, other than surveillance. But he did refer to it as having been "rigged for silent running." However, when he opened up the briefing to questions, and we asked him to describe what he meant by "rigged for silent running," he brushed the question aside. "You'll be getting that information after dinner," was all he said, "when you meet your instructors."

As we learned pretty quickly, the Major stuck to his guns.

He closed the briefing by telling us that the remaining members of our team would join us the next day. He described them as "a specially selected unit of highly trained professionals who would serve as our security force." Then he broke up the session, we returned to our rooms, washed, and were escorted to the cafeteria for our evening meal.

Being a field grade officer, the Major did not join us. We four humble technicians ate by ourselves in a cafeteria large enough to hold a hundred and fifty men, sitting awkwardly at a table under the scrutiny of an armed guard posted at either door. There was no way we could leave the cafeteria, let alone the building, without their consent, and their orders were to keep us under wraps—which was not a happy thought, despite our tendency to rationalize it as standard operating procedure.

As we ate, feigning indifference, the knowledge that our every move was being watched began to take its toll. Our table talk was stilted, limited to superficial speculation about the "advanced equipment" we would be "utilizing." We wondered what was meant by "rigged for silent running," but no one dared talk about the mission itself. If some omnipotent behavioral modification scientist had been observing us, he would have been pleased with our show of submission. Our masters already were playing us like musical instruments in a classical string quartet.

*   *   *

After dinner the tension generated by the heightened security was broken, to our relief, when we were finally introduced to our equipment. As this phase defined our role, I'll quickly describe the technology that made us integral parts of the mission.

We were brought back to the same classroom where we had met the Major. Again we were told to take seats and wait, and a few minutes later a young Air Force lieutenant entered from a side door that led to a storage room. Trailing behind him were four airmen carrying sound and camera equipment. Each airman gently laid his piece of equipment on the table and stood at ease behind it. The lieutenant introduced himself as being with intelligence, but our attention was riveted not on him but on the equipment, which was, in a word, fascinating.

"This is your equipment," the lieutenant said reverently. "It is the finest in the world, the state of the art. As you can see, there are four cameras for still pictures (his hand moved over them, as if casting a spell) and a video camera for cinematography. And then there is this extraordinary mini-dish and sound recording pack for intercepting voice communications."

We drew a collective breath in awe.

The lieutenant, having been briefed, knew exactly who we were. He indicated that Rusty and I would be taking still pictures with the four cameras, that Taurus would be handling the video equipment, and that José would be our soundman.

"Each of you will receive individual instruction in the piece of equipment you will be handling," he said, "but first we want to familiarize *all* of you with *all* of what we have. We want you to be capable of operating each other's equipment, just in case a situation arises in which that becomes necessary."

At that point an airman stepped forward and held the first of the four cameras on the table. I immediately recognized it as a standard, motor-driven Leica Mode M-2, as were the other three. Upon closer inspection, however, there was nothing standard about the cameras. The manufacturer's markings had been removed, and whereas most cameras are silver and black, these—including the lenses, carrying cases, attachments, and sound recording devices—had been camouflaged with green paint.

Holding the camera to his eye, the airman aimed it at the back wall and snapped an imaginary picture.

Now anyone familiar with motor-driven cameras knows how loud the sound is of a shutter opening and closing. But this camera made no noise whatsoever. Not a buzz or a whine or a click was heard. It was perfectly silent. As the Major termed it, "rigged for silent running."

How the silent running had been achieved was not something we technicians had a need to know. Our compartmented instruction was limited to utilization, so that particular aspect of our equipment's development was never explained. But it certainly required some sophisticated engineering.

Not only had the cameras been camouflaged and silenced, they had been modified in other significant respects as well. The film, for example. Commercial film is rated at 400 ASA, but the black and white 35mm film we were using had been specially treated, and was rated at 3200 ASA. That meant it would take four times less light to properly expose the film, enabling us to take pictures, at night, that had daylight quality and texture.

Another modification was the addition of "image intensifiers" inside the lenses. Again the engineering was not explained, but the end result was that the sensors allowed sufficient starlight and moonlight to pass through the lenses, so that we could see a bright green tinted field image. Essentially a visual aid, the image intensifiers helped us to see as clearly at night as during the day.

The cameras also had "doublers" built into their bodies between the light meters and lenses. These served to increase focal length. With a doubler attached, a 135mm lens had the focal capacity of a 270mm lens, and so on. The beauty of this feature was that it provided us with an extra margin of safety, by allowing us to stand further away from whatever it was we were watching.

Although no expense had been spared, the size and weight of the equipment could not be substantially modified in our favor. The Leicas were dinosaurs compared to what is available today, and without a lens attached, each one weighed about eight pounds, and they were bulky too. Plus which there were four lenses, one for each camera: a 24mm wide angle lens and a 105mm for Rusty; and a 500mm and a 200mm for me. Notably, the lenses did not screw onto the camera bodies but came equipped with "bayonet" mounts—little latches you clipped into place on the light meter, turned, and locked into place.

To compensate for the bulk, the carrying cases had been custom made for use in the jungle. Fabricated from a lightweight sturdy metal resembling Titanium (used to build airplane parts), each case was fashioned with molded, cushioned compartments so the camera bodies and attachments would not rattle or get damaged. The cases also were camouflaged, watertight, and rigged for silent running. Fully packed the entire ensemble weighed around twenty-five pounds. Affixed to the bottom of our rucksacks, the cases were to remain sealed until the moment the cameras were needed.

Taurus's video equipment was perhaps twice the size of a modern home movie camera. Weighing about thirty pounds it was, in essence, a rectangular box he balanced on his shoulder. Incidentally, the decision to use video, which was still in its infancy in 1967, was based on the concern that film in a movie camera might get tangled during the mission if it had to be removed in a hurry, whereas the videotape was contained in a cartridge inside an external component strapped to the operator's waist, and could be removed instantly and intact in an emergency.

Of all the equipment, José's was the most fascinating. The audio unit consisted of a camouflaged mini-dish, a plastic headset, and a camouflaged component housing the audiotape cassette. All of the parts were inter-connected with insulated wire. Approximately one foot in diameter, the mini-dish functioned like an antenna—albeit the smallest, most sensitive antenna any of us had ever seen. To use it, José simply aimed it at the people he wanted to monitor. The dish was wired to the headset so he could listen and make adjustments on the recording component he wore on his hip. The recording component resembled a modern tape recorder, but more solidly built, and lighter.

Our instruction lasted about four hours, first as a group, then with our individual instructors. During the individual portion of our instruction we each got a feel for what we personally would be handling. As a group we were shown how to properly load and unload, assemble and disassemble, and operate each piece of equipment.

My individual instruction required no adjustments in personal technique, but in view of the modifications that had been made, was intended to make sure I knew how to properly expose the film. The same applied to Rusty, who had the same basic equipment I had, and would be performing the same basic function, although from a different perspective. My lenses were marginally larger and heavier than his, while Taurus carried the heaviest load, and José carried the lightest.

The class ended around midnight with another practice session scheduled for the next day, at which time we were scheduled to use the equipment under simulated nighttime conditions. The equipment was put back in the storage room and we returned to our rooms feeling restless and excited. At last the mission was assuming a recognizable form. There were tangible things we could relate to, and we were feeling much better.

*   *   *

The following morning after breakfast we were taken to the basement, into a huge room specifically designed for testing night vision equipment. The ceiling was checkered with fluorescent lamps that the lieutenant regulated from a remote control switchboard, which enabled him to increase or decrease the light in any portion of the room, as he desired. We were positioned at one end with our instructors and we began taking pictures of, and in Jose's case recording the conversation of, a group of airmen at the other end.

It was the first time we had used such advanced equipment, but we quickly got accustomed to it. For best results I learned to set my shutter speed at $1/60^{th}$ of a second; then by turning the aperture dial until it aligned with the light meter setting, the camera automatically told me what F-Stop to use. It was that easy and by noon we all had effectively mastered the equipment.

We broke for lunch, at which point the film and tapes were sent out for processing. After lunch we spent the first part of the afternoon evaluating slides of the pictures that Rusty and I had taken. The results could not have been better. But the thing that impressed me the most (and which had nothing to do with my skills as a photographer, but was a result of the accelerated film speed, which literally froze the action), was the capacity of the cameras to take still shots of people in motion, without the images coming out blurred.

Next they put away the carousel, produced a television monitor, and analyzed the videotape Taurus had shot. Then they synchronized the videotape with José's audiotape. It was amazing, like watching a Hollywood movie, and we all received high praise from the lieutenant, who expressed profound relief that his coveted state-of-the-art equipment was in capable hands, and would be utilized to its maximum potential.

We tried to take the praise, and the sense of our self-importance that accompanied it, in stride; but starting at that moment there was a heightened awareness of the seriousness of our mission, and a growing awareness of our unproven ability to perform well together in the field.

For me that lingering doubt was a challenge that transcended the lure of easy money. For the first time in my life I felt that my thirst for adventure would finally be fulfilled.

The mission had become irresistible.

Chapter Four

That evening after dinner we returned to our rooms to find that the security team had arrived and settled into adjacent rooms in our secluded wing of the Special Operations facility. And with the security team came new doubts and suspicions, fostered by their callous and contemptuous attitude. Not one of them smiled or uttered a friendly word, or made even the slightest effort to introduce himself. With their presence, the TDY mission acquired an entirely new and sinister aspect.

We got a closer look at the security team about an hour later at another briefing in the classroom where we had first met the Major. There were seven of them, bringing the total number in our team to twelve. They were all older than me, ranging in age from their mid-twenties to their early thirties. All were dressed in plain green fatigues, and all wore the stone cold expression of professional soldiers bracing themselves for the next jolt of combat. From their jump boots we could tell they were US Army Airborne Rangers, making them America's best trained soldiers; mean and tough as nails, the type who get dropped in a jungle with a knife and compass and emerge three days later, relaxed and well rested.

The Major introduced each man mechanically, not by name but by the role he would play. He started with the Team Leader, whom he referred to as the Number One or, when he was feeling humanistic, as "Chief." The Major said the Team Leader would disseminate his orders from that point on. The Team Leader was about five ten, 145 pounds, raw-boned with sinewy muscles, medium brown hair, brown eyes, and enormous hands that looked twice as large as normal for a person his size.

The Number Two was skinny and nervous, and the Number Three had bad teeth and cruel eyes. The Gunner resembled Charles Atlas, while the Grenadier had the looks and mannerisms of Sammy Davis Junior. The team's Tracker was blond and handsome and very young, and appeared painfully shy. The Radioman/Medic was at least thirty, and although rugged and fit, had the puffy eyes and red veined nose of an episodic alcoholic.

I would never learn anything about them as individuals, but it was clear they shared one outstanding trait with our Major: each was a certifiable loner and, perhaps, a sociopath. As civilians they would be misfits. Their talent was war.

The briefing that night was as quick as it was uncomfortable, lasting maybe ten minutes; just long enough to meet the security team and learn that after collecting our survival gear and weapons, we would be flying the next day to Travis Air Force Base in California on the first leg of our journey. Before asking the Team Leader to break up the meeting, the Major did, however, present us with the camera and sound equipment, which we brought back to our rooms, packed and ready to go. If it didn't exactly belong to us it was, at least, in our possession, providing us with something solid to hold on to while our links with the real world rapidly began to slip away.

* * *

The next day we were awoken before dawn, served breakfast, told by the Team Leader to gather our camera and sound equipment, and then driven in a canvass covered truck to the base dispensary where we were given a series of booster shots.

Following that we were taken to a secure area inside a warehouse where we exchanged the clothes we were wearing for green fatigues. Our fifteen-o-fives were packed in cardboard boxes, tagged, and interred in footlockers. We were handed a camouflaged rucksack to which we technicians attached our carrying cases. We also received a single pair of camo fatigues, a poncho and liner, a boonie hat, a green towel, socks, underwear, two canteens, camo stick, insect repellent, toilet paper, water purification and salt pills, foot powder, buffed Seiko wristwatches which we strapped on, tiny dime sized compasses with buffed surfaces and a nylon cord so we could wear them around our necks, survival matches, and the obligatory Swiss army knife.

Doc, the radioman/medic, drew a supply of medicines, wound dressings, antiseptics, morphine syringes, uppers and downers, and assorted medical supplies. He also received his radio, an upgraded version of the standard PRC-25.

A crate of pre-packaged food was brought forth, as well as crates of ammunition. We each received a brand new M-16, a BAR belt for magazines, a brand new Browning semi-automatic with holster and belt, and a serrated survival knife and sheath. Atlas drew a short-barreled M-60 machine gun and about twenty bandoleers of 50 caliber ammunition, which were packed in a crate. Sammy the Grenadier drew an M-79 grenade launcher, which the other security people referred to as his "pirate pistol." It was a nasty looking breech loading weapon that resembled Steve McQueen's sawed-off shotgun in *Wanted: Dead Or Alive*. The pirate pistol fired spin-stabilized 40mm high explosive (HE), gas and buckshot grenades. Sammy drew about sixty HE rounds, about fifteen buckshot rounds, and about six gas grenades, all of which he stuffed in an olive green sack and put in a crate along with enough fragmentation and concussion grenades to supply each man in the team with six apiece. A dozen Claymore mines were crated, as were four extra M-16s. M-16 magazines were plentiful, perhaps as many as forty per man. The Team Leader knew the exact number and checked every item off a list.

There also was a box whose contents we were not permitted to see. This surprise package was personally inspected and packed by the Team Leader, off in a corner.

Simply stated, the magnitude of our arsenal was out of this world. And while not inconsistent with what a typical recon team might carry, it certainly cast doubt on what we had been told about the degree of risk involved in the mission. Indeed when we asked, "What's with all the armaments?", we were told: "It's just a precaution." A perfunctory response that did little to allay our anxieties.

Under the direction of the Team Leader we were driven to a Small Arms Range, where sample ammunition was distributed, and where we sighted and test fired our weapons. As I mentioned earlier, I had graduated at the top of my basic training class in hand-to-hand combat and armaments, and although I was out of practice, I shot the eyes out of the targets—an accomplishment that endeared me to the M-60 gunner, Atlas, who said I should have been Infantry instead of "pretty pictures."

Rusty, José, and Taurus were not nearly as proficient as I, so from that point on the security people tended to treat me as the de-facto leader of our clumsy sub-culture. I had gained a degree of respect, to the point where Atlas asked to see what I could do with the precious M-60 he cuddled like a baby in his massive arms. Just for the fun of it I popped off a few rounds; and I must admit, there was a sobering and foreboding sense of power in handling such a dangerous weapon.

The weapons all checked out fine and we returned to the warehouse where our camera and sound equipment, rucksacks packed with survival gear, and crates full of weapons, ammunition, and supplies were tagged and prepared for shipping. The crates were loaded into a waiting flatbed truck and driven to a corner of Hurlburt Field, and we boarded a C-130 transport and were flown to Travis Air Force Base in California.

Things were starting to happen a little too fast for comfort, and we technicians were starting to feel a little like prisoners. We were the only passengers aboard the plane and throughout the flight the security people watched our every move, listened to every word we said, and resorted to every means short of physical intimidation to inhibit us.

*   *   *

Located about forty miles north of San Francisco, Travis Air Force Base is the main departure point for all western bound Air Force transport planes. We arrived at "the gateway to the Pacific" at about dinnertime and were taken directly to a restricted barracks where, under the scrutiny of the security people, we washed, ate, returned to our cots, and slept. The following morning we boarded a DC-9 filled exclusively with Air Force personnel heading to Southeast Asia. There were no civilians on board, and the twelve members of our team were strategically seated together at the front of the plane, technicians interspersed among the vigilant security people, to prevent us from lapsing into unauthorized conversations.

The flight was dreary and boring, filled with dull girly magazines, an enforced silence, and the restiveness and discomfort of long distance travel.

Seventeen hours later, after a stopover in Hawaii, we landed at Clark Air Force Base in the Philippines. Our backs were stiff and sore and we were eager to disembark. Looking out the windows we could see the heat waves rising from the tarmac, and even before they opened the doors we could smell the pungent odors of the tropical vegetation. It was about 2:00pm, the hottest time of the day, when we stepped into the vicious heat and humidity.

With the Major observing, the Team Leader led us to a flat bed truck that had a wooden bench along each side, a canvass top, and an open back. Our equipment had been shipped separately on another flight and was already stacked inside. The security people were unhappy that strangers had handled their possessions, and were anxious to examine the crates and ascertain that everything had arrived intact. There was an American driver and a Filipino seated beside him, both regular Army. The twelve of us climbed in the back, sitting six on each side with the gear at our feet, then proceeded to drive through the airbase gates into the flat green countryside and choking haze.

The drive was quite an experience. We had been told that our mission was in the Philippines so I tried to be as observant as possible. After about ten minutes we rolled up the canvass sides to improve the ventilation, and from what I saw of the countryside, the Filipinos had a lower standard of living than the impoverished Mexicans living, if you can call it living, in the squalid ghettos of Juarez. There wasn't, however, the virulent anti-Americanism one found in Mexican border towns. On the contrary, the Filipino kids waved at our truck and from what I was told, the average Filipino welcomed Americans.

Be that as it may, it is a fact that most American serviceman stationed in the Philippines were content with the status quo. Their paltry military pay was equivalent to the minimum wage in America, but the Yankee dollar stretched a lot further in the Philippines, and the imbalance in the rate of exchange allowed servicemen to live a lifestyle that was otherwise beyond their reach. If they grew accustomed to the climate and culture, some decided to capitalize on their pensions, and settled there upon retiring.

Right away I wondered if this lop-sided arrangement wasn't the reason for our mission? Surely, I conjectured, there must be an insurrection smoldering somewhere in the hills. Maybe we did need the guns after all?

As Clark faded into the distance, the Team Leader told us that we were heading to a military installation about two hours away. He said we would bivouac there overnight, then fly out early the next morning to our final destination. Wiping the sweat from our faces, we listened passively while he explained how we would be isolated from the other

Americans on duty at this installation, and that if anyone asked, we were to say we were "on maneuvers."

As usual our masters were feeding us information piecemeal, so as not to reveal the true object of the mission. The Team Leader did, however, assure us that everything was going as planned.

For the first hour we traveled on a paved road. There was a cooler of ice water to soothe our parched throats, but other than passing the cooler around, the trip passed in relative silence. The security people were eager to make sure their weapons had arrived intact, and the stress of the plane ride had made them crankier than usual. If it was necessary for one of them to address one of us technicians, it was invariably, "Hey, you."

To occupy myself and compensate for their unpleasant behavior, I contrived dumb nicknames (based on their most obvious characteristics) for the three as yet unchristened security people. The team's Number Two, with his Brooklyn accent and a lexicon rife with "youse guys" and "dees tings," became Joey, after the renowned New York City mobster Joey Gallo. Our sadistic Number Three became Johnny Reb (aka Reb) because his accent placed him below the Mason Dixon Line. And our bashful Tracker, who sat quietly beside the Major, became Davy, after my hero Davy Crockett, the king of the wild frontier who died so magnificently at the Alamo.

Compiling this glossary of names did not take long (or much imagination), and by the time I had finished we had turned onto a gravel road and were heading into the hills. A series of Keep Out signs warned of our approach to the military installation, prompting everyone to take heed. We were stopped at and passed through several chain link gates manned by heavily armed Filipino soldiers, until finally we were admitted to a well maintained but small airbase, with three hangars and a short airstrip.

The airbase itself was a Filipino Special Forces training camp. There were Filipino soldiers and civilians moving around, along with a smattering of US Army Special Forces advisors. There were also regular US Army and Air Force personnel. Any Navy SEALS or Force Recon Marines in the Philippines would have been down at Subic Bay with the Seventh Fleet.

It was late afternoon when we rumbled into camp. We dropped the Major off first at the base commander's post, where, exercising his rights to privacy and privilege, he would commiserate with his management peers. The rest of us, being labor, were driven to an empty sealed compound composed of several canvass tents pitched on raised wooden platforms. We offloaded our crates and stacked them in the squad tent we would be sharing. The truck departed and American guards sealed the compound.

Looking around the compound I could see a combination mess and recreation tent with a picnic table, benches, card table, and transistor radio tuned to the local US Army station. The disc jockey was playing Country Western music. I wished he was playing rock & roll, and I wished that I were back at Foley's Bar & Grill, dropping a quarter in the jukebox. Showers and toilets were outdoors. We could smell the base's evening meal being prepared and when we asked about it, the Team Leader said that our meals would be brought to us.

Meanwhile there were important things to do. The Team Leader had us double-check and load our weapons, and then he marched us over to the base rifle range to test them again. All had arrived in good condition and we returned to our tent to organize our survival gear. The Team Leader had us change into our camo fatigues, repack our rucksacks with our carrying cases attached, and then he made us jump off the raised platform to make sure the ensemble was noise and rattle proof.

As we finished that exercise a sudden downpour sent people around the base scurrying inside the mess hall. The wind picked up, branches and debris whipped through the air, and there were booming claps of thunder as we plodded through muddy puddles to the mess tent in our compound. Our supper was brought to us in pre-heated vacuum-sealed containers by a Filipino mess crew, each course arriving in a separate tub. One was full of chunks of beef and gravy, another with tasteless mashed potatoes, another with sad string beans. We served ourselves, glumly passing around stacks of plates and cups, and handfuls of utensils. There was a refrigerated case with cans of soda and milk containers. For dessert we had chocolate cake with soggy frosting, and a choice of tea or coffee. I tell you this because it felt like our last supper, and there was no conversation worth repeating. The security people were busy winding their internal main springs, and they ate very little. I found their lack of appetite disconcerting, but I'm hungry under any circumstances so I ate my full. In another corner of the squad tent, Doc and Sammy sipped cups of coffee, discussed their wicked ex-wives, and chain-smoked Pall Malls. The rain stopped, the bugs attacked, and everything smelled like decay.

The Filipinos returned and gathered up our mess, and while they did that I slipped off to the latrine with Taurus. Sitting side-by-side and whispering, we deliberated on the issues at hand, and determined that the security people had higher security clearances than we did and, subsequently, had a much better idea of what was going on. Taurus thought the mission probably was directed against American servicemen stealing guns from an airbase, or something to that effect. We agreed that his theory made more sense than my theory about insurgents. But we did not know what the mission was all about, and we felt we needed to know because of the emphasis on armaments and security, so we decided to ask the Team Leader directly. As the acknowledged leader of our little subgroup, the honor of broaching the subject, when the time was right, fell on my shoulders.

Back at the squad tent we found the security people cleaning their weapons yet again. We were told to do the same. Breaking open the ammo crate, the Team Leader began handing out clips to everyone. He told us to remove the last three rounds and replace them with two tracers. The reason, he explained, was twofold; so we would know during a firefight when our magazine was empty, and because M-16s had a tendency to jam when fully loaded.

Attention to such detail reconfirmed what we already deduced; that the situation we were heading into was far more dangerous than we had been told. The tent smelled of gun oil and imminent combat. Taurus had relayed our plan to Rusty and José, and I felt their eyes drilling into me. It was time to take the plunge.

"Chief," I said, getting his and everyone else's attention. "Me and the other guys would like to know what the story is. Now that we're about to go, will you fill us in?"

"What you worried about, boy," Reb drawled. "We well armed, ain't we?"

His remark elicited caustic chuckles, grunts, and snorts of agreement from the other security people. Offended by my presumptions, the Team Leader simply ignored me altogether.

"What about it, Chief?" I asked again.

Laying his weapon across his lap and looking at me with premeditated scorn, he said, "What the hell makes you think I'd tell you, even if I knew?"

Now, I've never backed down from a fight in my life. I'd even punched out a barracks sergeant in Biloxi, who was rummaging through my stuff looking for pot. That's why I was transferred to New Mexico. And although I knew the Team Leader could take me apart in a fight, I also knew that backing down now would psychologically destroy me. If I backed down now, I would lose, forever, the small measure of status I had attained, so I pressed the issue.

"Listen, Chief," I said respectfully, but looking him straight in the eye. "I'm not looking for trouble. But we're the ones that got suckered into this thing, not you. We're not about to turn around. You know we can't. We just want you to level with us, that's all."

The Team Leader considered what I had said, and done. "You four people are important to us," he said candidly. "We can't pull this thing off without you. So just relax and remember; we'll do whatever it takes to get you through. Okay?"

It wasn't exactly what we wanted to hear, but it was good enough for the time being. "Okay, Chief," I said, then leaned back on my cot and tried to clear my mind.

*   *   *

Later that night the Major materialized in our tent, to assure himself that we were mentally and emotionally prepared for the mission, and to reiterate, abstrusely, the itinerary he had planned. He said we would be flying to our final destination early the next day, but its location would remain unspecified until we were in the air. He seemed wide-awake and in high spirits. I wondered if he ever slept.

The Major asked the Team Leader if all systems were go, and nodded contentedly when told they were.

"Hit the sack and get a good night's sleep," he said, then left without further adieu, fading into the shadows where he lurked, remote and unmoved.

Chapter Five

The suffocating fear that would accompany me for the next four days, and haunt me for the rest of my life, surfaced that night in the Philippines.

It started as self-reproach. As I lay on my cot I knew we were being deceived, but I blamed myself, not the Major or anyone else. I blamed myself because I had broken the cardinal rule of enlisted men: I'd volunteered. I'd succumbed to the lure of easy money and the thrill of traveling overseas on a secret mission that was supposedly safe. But now that my eyes were opening, I could see just how gullible I'd been. I cursed my stupidity.

Then I got mad at the military. The security team knew what was happening and were prepared for the worst. The Major certainly knew how dangerous the mission was going to be. And with that realization I was overcome by dread. I realized how small and easily misplaced our little team really was. All our bridges had been burned and not a caring soul knew where we were.

At 4:00am, as the Team Leader roused us from our restless sleep, the Major illuminated the squad tent with his ectoplasmic presence. He asked the Team Leader to get us up and going. In the distance we could hear the whine of an airplane warming its engines. Without pausing to eat we strapped on our gear, cradled our weapons, and made for the plane. The crates with our supplies, ammunition, and extra weapons were loaded on a truck and driven to the airstrip by American members of the base security unit. In the early morning twilight I could see the outline of a C-130. It was painted brown and green and the windows were painted black. There were no markings on the plane, but a row of silver antennas stuck out of its upper body, not far behind the cockpit, like hackles on an animal's back. The flight crew looked ghostly in metallic gray jumpsuits and the reflected glow of their flashlights, as they inspected the undercarriage of the aircraft in the dissipating darkness.

We had never seen a C-130 like it, and while the crates were being carried off the truck and up the ramp into the rear of the plane, Taurus sidled up to me and asked, "What the fuck is going on? Why the hell are the windows painted black?"

"I've got no idea," I replied. But the time for playing patsy was over.

In the military, questions from an enlisted man to an officer are always channeled through a non-commissioned officer like our Team Leader. Not doing so violates the sacred chain of command and is tantamount to insubordination. But I approached the Major and asked him directly, "What's going on, sir? Why are the windows painted black?"

The Major had just finished speaking with the Team Leader, who shot me a look laden with malice. The Major motioned him inside the plane, then said reassuringly, "Don't worry. It's just a security precaution, so the aircraft can fly into classified areas at night without being seen. That's all." And with that he turned on his heels and walked up the ramp.

In a state of disbelief, Taurus, Rusty, José and I dumbly followed them up the ramp, and were told by the aggravated Team Leader to park ourselves on either side of the crates in the rear of the plane. It was eerie inside the stripped-down C-130, like being inside the skeleton of some psychedelic Moby Dick. The steel super-structure was dimly visible in the glow of small red, green, and white lights. Rows of seats lined the sides, and running down the middle was a static jump line. A curtain separated us from the flight crew and whatever electronic spy gear the Air Force Security Service people were operating up front.

The ramp was raised, sealing our fate. A red light came on warning us to fasten our seat belts. We were ready for take off and the moment of truth had arrived. As if he were about to address the Tuesday night meeting of the local Rotary Club, the Major stood up and broke the bad news.

"There's been a change in our plans," he said casually.

Four mouths simultaneously fell open.

Noting our distress, but indifferent to it, the Major continued. "We're not staying in the Philippines. Instead we're going into an undisclosed area in Southeast Asia. We'll be in the air for about six hours, so just relax." Then he sat down without offering any further explanation.

I looked at my watch. It was 5:00am. What time zone would we be entering? Rusty nudged me. "Pete. What are we getting ourselves into?"

I took it as a rhetorical question and shook my head. Whatever we were heading into, I should have known better. As a photojournalist I distorted the facts everyday. But there I was, trapped by my own greed. So I told myself it wasn't personal, that they were lying to us for our own good, that it was just the usual military bullshit.

But as we would soon learn, all too well, it wasn't the usual bullshit at all.

Propelled by its jet assists, the C-130 rumbled down the runway then roared into the level light of dawn, heading for places unknown.

*   *   *

Shortly after we were airborne, a member of the flight crew served us vacuum- sealed meals consisting of preheated plates of scrambled eggs, bacon, sausage, and toast. We were given cups of coffee too, and those of us who had appetites ate. Afterwards we were handed a deck of cards. To amuse ourselves we played gin rummy on the ammo crate that had been our breakfast table. There was little conversation and our intermittent griping was met with icy stares and exhortations from the security team to, "Knock it off!" Which we eventually did, as our resentment dissolved into bitter resignation. The 1966 Christmas edition of *Playboy* was passed around, but only Reb showed any interest. For the most part the security people were busy making last minute adjustments in their gear, tying loose pieces of equipment to their camo fatigues, taping the cuffs of their pants to their boots, and that sort of thing.

Halfway through the flight the Team Leader opened the small box containing the security team's private stash of exotic weaponry. Inside were wire garrotes, plastic handcuffs, and tiny hand-held, trigger-operated crossbows that shot four-inch long, poison tipped arrows. Also inside were lethal daggers with blades barely an inch wide, but razor sharp on both sides and tapered to a point with a single purpose. These were removed with pride and sharpened with loving care on an oiled whetstone by the four security people who were destined to use them: the Team Leader, Reb, Joey, and Davy, who didn't seem quite so innocent or bashful anymore.

While these regimens were being performed, three shanghaied photographers and one sorry soundman sat in foreboding silence, surrounded in their estimation by seven homicidal maniacs. Our Team Leader with his Gerber, garrote, and crossbow was the one man you knew Mr. D would avoid. Atlas had two bandoleers of M-60 ammo wrapped around his body-builder's torso, and a sanguinary expression on his face. Sammy with his yellow eyes, gold tooth, and pirate pistol was twitching with nervous energy. Then there was Reb; you just knew that Reb loved to torment little animals, and would have been laboring on an Alabama chain gang if the military hadn't grabbed him first. Joey, the hood, certainly felt right at home with our gang. Doc, our world-weary radioman-medic, was dreaming of cigarettes and tall cold beers. And Davy—Davy was just a clean-cut country boy who would return to his family and never utter a word about what he had done for God and Country, assuming he survived.

Oh, and last but not least there was our mighty, enigmatic Major, one part fact, one part apparition.

* * *

At 10:00am sandwiches and coffee were served and for the first time in my life I had indigestion. I decided it was a side effect of the anti-malaria pills, not nervousness, but in either case I felt queasy and flushed and found myself sitting on the john. My palms were sweating and my hands were shaking when I got back to my seat.

At 10:45 we were told to strap on our gear and prepare to disembark. José was praying and crossing himself. Tears had welled up in Rusty's eyes. Taurus leaned over and whispered, "I've been doing some figuring Pete, and it doesn't add up."

"What doesn't add up?" I inquired irritably.

"We've been in the air six hours. At three hundred twenty-five knots, that's about two thousand miles. According to my calculations, that puts us smack in the middle of fucking China…if we're flying in a straight line."

"Forget about it, man," I said. "They've been leading us in circles ever since we started. It's like the Navy. No one takes longer to cross the ocean than the Navy."

"Fuck it," Taurus said. "This whole thing is too…" His voice trailed off. "It's too fucking clandestine. And it stinks," he said a little louder.

"Take it easy," the Team Leader growled, looking at his watch. "Everyone set your watches at exactly thirteen hundred hours, fifty-five minutes." He counted down from ten and after he got to one, he said, "Now," and everybody knew what to do.

"Now listen up," he said. "The Major has something to say."

Looking as calm as a commuter whose train was pulling into Pleasantville, the Major stood up said, "Okay, people. In a few minutes we'll be landing in an area that's behind enemy lines. It's going to look a little primitive, but remember, you'll be looking pretty strange to these people too. They're local tribesmen, and they'll be assisting us on the mission. Stay loose, and do what you're told."

With that the Major sat down and the plane literally dropped like a stone. It was the most rapid descent of my life. My stomach did a triple flip and my ears popped. I held onto my seat and gulped mouthfuls of air to keep my eardrums from bursting.

Ten seconds later we touched ground. The windows were painted black so we couldn't see where we were, but from the way we bounced around we knew it wasn't on tarmac. It was the roughest landing I'd ever made. At the end of the runway the C-130 turned around and came to a halt with its engines running. As we unfastened our seat belts the Team Leader warned us to, "Keep your mouths shut and your fingers off your triggers."

The flight crew lowered the ramp and a brilliant light flooded the interior of the plane, temporarily blinding me. As my eyes adjusted, I followed the spectral shapes of the Major and security people off the plane. It was like stepping out of a Time Machine into the Stone Age.

"Oh my God," I thought. "Where the hell are we?"

The scene I beheld was totally captivating. Hypnotic. We had set down on a grass-covered runway that had been carved out of a mountaintop. The runway was about a thousand yards long, with both ends bordering steep cliffs. Cool breezes swept across our faces and in every direction we could see mist swirling around other mountains. It wasn't nearly as hot as the Philippines, but the vegetation was thick down below in the valleys. We were in the midst of a lush mountainous jungle, although where we stood, the trees and shrubs appeared to have been ripped out of the earth by explosions. And spread-out across the landing strip, about fifty feet away, was a company-sized outfit of fearsome Montagnard warriors. They were armed to the teeth with American weapons, but there wasn't a white face to be seen. No women or children either, just soldiers, some of who were nursing recent wounds.

We had stepped right into the middle of a war zone.

While the flight crew quickly off-loaded our crates, the co-pilot checked the undercarriage and the landing gear for damage. The security people deployed in a semi-circle around us while the Major entered into a conversation with the bearded chief of the tribe. They spoke in broken English and a few monosyllabic grunts, and then ducked into a nearby hut.

Satisfied the plane was still in one piece, the co-pilot and flight crew climbed back in and without uttering a work of encouragement or farewell they took off, leaving our little group to fend for ourselves. We were, in a word, stranded.

Suddenly it was very quiet. I felt vulnerable and exposed. One hundred and fifty Montagnard warriors closed to within ten feet of us, greedily examining our weapons and equipment, sizing us up, sending a message with their eyes that said, "Beware!"

I got the distinct feeling they had no love for dear old Uncle Sam, and for the first time I was grateful we had the security team to protect us. There was a lot of posturing going on, but the security people stood their ground like rocks, shooting a telepathic message right back at the Montagnards, one that said, "If you're feeling froggy, motherfucker, then jump!"

The Montagnards were disciplined enough not to provoke a confrontation. But I can still see their brutish faces and feel their black eyes exploring the fear in my heart. No disrespect intended, but they were the most animalistic human beings I had ever encountered. Most of them were wearing torn, loose-fitting, filthy US Army fatigues. Their teeth were black and rotten from chewing a root that got them high. The juice dribbled down their chins onto their chests. To the man they were dark skinned and stocky, less than five feet tall in most cases, with uncombed hair and gnarled hands and feet—products of an elemental environment that had hammered their minds and bodies into a fierce state of readiness.

My apprehension was reaching an all-time high, but subsided when I saw our dignified Major emerge from the hut with the bearded chieftain and his young, deferential lieutenant. They joined us where the crates had been stacked on the side of the landing strip. The chieftain spoke and the Major translated.

We were being assigned six bearers and four guides who reported to the Team Leader, who also spoke a few words of their Montagnard dialect.

Next the crates were broken open. The extra ammunition was packed in rucksacks, one each for two bearers. Two other bearers shouldered our food, and two more carried our water jugs. Each of the Montagnards draped a bandoleer of M-60 ammo over his shoulders, and each one of the four guides was handed a new M-16 and a dozen clips. They accepted and examined the weapons like professional soldiers, with pleasure.

Our team was assembled and we were led to a corner of the encampment where a square hut stood on short stilts. It had a steep thatched roof and sides that were rolled up and tied off with straw. Inside were damp reed mats. By then it was 3:00pm. Time, the Major said, to get some rest. He was about to return to the main encampment, without further explanation, when I found myself addressing him directly again.

"Major," I blurted out. "What's going on?"

Patiently he faced me, his arms akimbo. "Tonight," he said. "Tonight you'll learn everything." And with that he departed.

Chapter Six

Stunned by the stark reality of our predicament; that's how Rusty, Taurus, José and I felt as we unstrapped our gear and asked each other the obvious question: "Where the hell are we?"

Finding amusement in our confusion and distress, Doc knelt down in front of us and asked impishly, "So, you really want to know where you are?"

"Yeah," Taurus said recklessly. "Why don't you tell us where the fuck we are?"

"Yeah. Why don't you tell him, Doc," Reb said shrilly, mockingly. "We don't want no dissension among the troops now, do we?"

Doc looked down at the dirty wooden floor, chuckled, then cleared his throat and fixed us with a somber stare. "Well you boys are guests of the Sedang, the fiercest of the Montagnard warriors. These little bastards know nothing but fighting and killing, if you know what I mean?"

We stared back, not knowing what he meant, and not sure whether to believe him.

Doc asked us, "Would you sorry sons-of-bitches like to know what the Major is doing right now?" At this point even the security people drew closer, their rapt attention leading credence to what the grisly veteran was about to say.

Lowering his voice to a raspy whisper, our radioman-medic said, "Right this minute the Major's taking the blood oath with the Sedang chieftain, the bearded one who's in charge here. The Yards call it "xep" and its done to forge an alliance, or in this case, to strengthen one that's already made."

Atlas looked quizzically at the Team Leader for verification. An acknowledged authority, his eyes said, "Yes," what we were hearing was factual.

"That's right," Doc continued. "The Major's eating the sacrificial chicken and drinking rice beer from the sacred jar. Only there's not just beer in that jar." He laughed. "No, them Yards put a little blood in it too. Each man taking the oath has got to cut his finger and let the blood drip into the jar. Then the sorcerer adds some dried human bone for strength, and some deer horn and tiger's teeth, and bark from sacred trees and plants and vines. And a copper bracelet," Doc held up his arm, "like this, for good luck."

"Jesus," Taurus blurted out. "That's disgusting."

I conjured up visions of the witches in MacBeth.

"May be sick to you, boy," Doc muttered indignantly, "but not to them Yards. And for your information, if the Major didn't drink it, it would be an insult to the ghosts of all their ancestors...and your fat fucking head would be stuck on the end of a fucking pole. Understand?"

Reb giggled, and Taurus recoiled at the thought.

"There's a drink master," Doc explained, "who hands a straw to them that drinks. The sacred jar is marked on the inside with rings, and each man sucks up his share as the jar's passed around. No man's allowed to drink more than his share."

"Who the hell would want to," José laughed nervously.

"Don't make the mistake of looking down on these gooks," Doc grumbled. "These are some of the baddest asses in the world. You accidentally step on one of their taboos, and they'll eat your liver for supper."

Having issued that warning, Doc slipped down on his mat, hands behind his head, his lecture concluded. The security people dispersed, leaving only the Team Leader. He looked at us impatiently and said, "Enough of this useless fucking chatter. Get yourselves together now. Have your packs ready. Put something in you stomachs and take a shit outside. And get some rest."

That sounded like good advice so I laid back and listened to the weird sounds of Montagnard voices coming from their encampment. And while I lay there I went through a metamorphosis. As I looked around and saw nothing I could relate to, I realized that I had no one to rely upon, ultimately, but myself. Self-preservation became my one and only concern. And as I retreated deep within myself, I was overcome by a profound sense of equanimity. I knew that whatever came along, I could handle it. I found myself thinking, "I'm going to get out of here. I don't know how, but whatever I have to do, I'm going to get out of here alive."

My determination was complete. I knew I was going to survive.

No longer annoyed by the security people, I observed their behavior and realized it was rooted in the same survivor's instinct. My opinion of them was rapidly changing, and I decided the most intelligent thing I could do was copy them: watch them, study them, and pattern my feelings and actions on theirs. If they didn't want to talk to anyone or call anyone by name, then the same went for me. What mattered now was controlling my emotions, conserving my strength, and keeping my eyes wide open.

Although the fear and apprehension would never completely disappear, they did subside, and I found comfort in the single-mindedness that would be my saving grace. Once I knew I could make it, no matter what happened to everyone else, I was able to relax and eventually fall asleep.

* * *

It was chilly when the Team Leader awakened us. It was dark too and the hands on my luminous wristwatch said 3:30am. Sometime during the night the thatched sides of our hut had been lowered to keep out the cold mountain air, as well as the noise from the boisterous ceremony in the Montagnard leader's hut. One of our guides had started a fire in a clay stove in a corner of the hut, and the firelight cast a flickering glow on our bodies and faces. Streams of acrid wood smoke drifted inside the hut, and the larger than life shadows of men rising from sleep did a macabre dance on the thatched walls enveloping us. Outside the entire outpost was shrouded in darkness.

Kneeling in the center of the hut was our charismatic Major. "Gather round me men," he whispered.

We huddled around him like a football team. Not a soul was stirring in the Montagnard camp. It was so quiet we could hear each other breathing.

"Is the team's gear together, Chief?" the Major asked.

"Yes, sir," came the confidant reply.

"Good. In a few minutes our guides will begin to lead us on a three-day patrol into a region approximately thirty kilometers from here. This morning we'll move down the side of the mountain to the village below where their families are living."

He spoke purposefully but introspectively, as if lost in a trance. "You'll find the going gets tougher as we move along the ridge, and even tougher tomorrow when we cross the valley to the other side. On Day Three we'll head due west across a plateau to our objective. Moving will be easier once we're on the plateau…what we call the Golf Course."

The Major's eyes were glazed, the pupils dilated from intoxicants. His eyes fell on mine. "I want the photographers and the soundman to pay particularly close attention to what I am about to say." His gaze shifted from me to José, then Rusty, then Taurus, then back to me. "We're going to be surveiling an area where there are suspected drug dealings. We believe there are fields where poppies are grown and then processed into opium. We believe Americans may be involved. Americans with the CIA."

Someone whistled softly between his teeth.

"We're going in to find out if this is the case," the Major continued, "and if it is, we're bringing back the evidence."

Removing a photograph from his breast pocket (I noticed his finger had been cut), the Major said in a low tone of voice, "I want the four of you to take a good look at the man in this picture. His name is Jason. Remember that: Mr. Jason."

The name hung suspended in the air like holograph. Mr. Jason.

Handing the photo to me, the Major said, "Pass it around."

In order to see Mr. Jason's face clearly, I had to tip the photograph so it caught the firelight from the hearth. What I saw was an elderly man with thinning gray hair, small features, and glasses. He was wearing a gray business suit and a tie. He looked like anybody's distinguished grandfather. Mr. Jason.

I handed the photo to José and it made the rounds. Everyone took a look, including the security people. It came back to me and I passed it to the Major. He seemed a million miles away, floating on some placid inner lake. "If anything should happen to me," he said stoically, "this is the man you will deliver the film to. You will not give the film to anyone else, nor, under any circumstances whatsoever will you reveal to anyone but Mr. Jason what is on the film, or how you got it. That is an order. Do you understand?"

Murmured yessirs came from every direction but his eyes were on mine. It was like I was being initiated into the inner circle of some secret cult. I didn't want to break the spell.

Then a wry smile transformed the Major's mystical countenance. His eyes began to blaze and the brightening hut seemed to resonate from some fervent chord of defiance he had struck at the core of his being.

"Good," he said, striking a match on a matchbox handed to him by Doc, then setting the photograph in his hand on fire. "Then say "Goodbye" to Mr. Jason."

He smiled demonically as he watched it dissolve into smoke and ash.

And in the sublime silence that ensued I knew the Major had signed his own death warrant. I felt a sudden flash of pity, then awe, then aversion. He was a marked man. Stay away.

Reverting to his usual demeanor, composed and aloof, the Major spoke again with conviction. "From here on out there will be no more questions." Again he looked at me. "No more talk. It's time to get serious."

There were mumbled grunts of assent from the security team.

Enunciating each syllable so there would be no mistaking his meaning, the Major said: "From now on we'll be communicating with hand signals. No smoking either. Stay five paces apart, one eye on the man in front of you and the other eye on the ground. Don't get separated. Listen, but don't be concerned by every sound you hear."

He paused, the emptiness asking if there were any questions. There were none.

Rising to his feet the Major said in soldierly fashion, "Form them up, Chief. It's time to move out. We'll eat when we reach the village."

"Okay everybody," the Team Leader said, assuming command. "Make sure you've got everything. Don't forget nothing." He circulated among us, checking our equipment, and when he was satisfied that all was in order, he showed us how to apply our camo paint. "Like this," he said, rubbing the stick in his palms then spraying insect repellant on top of it, working the mixture into his oversized hands, and smearing it on his face. We did likewise.

The Yards were waiting outside, squatting on their haunches, enjoying one last cigarette. The Team Leader pow-wowed with our four bow-legged guides. Their names were Dil, Song, Klun, and Pring, and together with the Chief they walked over to a break in the outpost's perimeter where a downhill path began.

One by one the Team Leader tapped us on the shoulder, lining us up in the formation he wanted. We were divided into three groups. Group One was composed of Dil, Davy, the Team Leader, the Major, me and two bearers. Group Two consisted of Pring, Joey, two bearers, Atlas, Doc, José and Taurus. Group Three included Klun, Reb, Rusty, two bearers, and Sammy and Song pulling up the rear. Twenty-two men bonded by the secret we shared and the challenge of a three-day hike through enemy territory, to spy on suspected drug smugglers. Twenty-two men connected by a strange amalgamation of science and superstition. Twenty-two men stepping into the abyss.

Having the advantage of hindsight, I can now sketch that abyss. To the east, from South Vietnam's Central Highlands, came American reconnaissance and counter-terror teams, led to the Ho Chi Minh trails by Montagnard scouts like ours. To the west were the relatively useless Royal Lao Armed Forces, augmented by an aggressive Secret Army of Montagnards under General Vang Pao. Trained and directed by the CIA, the Secret Army worked out of Laotian towns like Pakse and Savvankhet, most of which were strung out along the Mekong River.

Enemy forces composed of the Communist Pathet Lao and their allies in the North Vietnamese Army (NVA), controlled the countryside in between South Vietnam's border with Southern Laos, and the Laotian towns that sat astride the Mekong River. It was through this area on the Bolovens Plateau, in the Laotian Panhandle, that we would be passing. The indigenous people inhabiting this area were known as the Lao Theung. Erstwhile members of the southern branch of the CIA's Secret Army of Montagnards, the Lao Theung had switched allegiances so many times that no one knew which side they were on anymore. Mostly they fought for the side that paid the highest price for their opium and, as the Major had explained, in the spring of 1967 the Lao Theung were doing business with the CIA.

Flying high above the fracas were F-4 Phantom jets on bombing runs, and C-130's flying daily reconnaissance missions over the Ho Chi Minh trails. The C-130 spy planes monitored all electronic communications in the region, and apparently one of those intercepted conversations was responsible for launching our mission. It's my guess that the intercepted conversation pinpointed the exact time and location of the drug transaction we were hoping to capture on film and tape.

Of course, there is always the possibility that someone on the inside had informed. But in either case, what happened to us had nothing to do with how the mission was generated.

Chapter Seven

In the spring of 1967 I was five feet seven inches tall, weighed 155 pounds, and was in excellent physical condition; which was fortunate because our Montagnard guides set a fast pace going down the hill. The billygoat path we used was well worn, smooth, steep and narrow, and it was hard keeping my balance. The pull of gravity forced me to lean back and shift my weight to my knees to keep from pitching forward headfirst. The last thing I wanted was to slip. The temperature was around sixty-five degrees, but the exertion generated additional heat. As the straps of my backpack bit into my shoulders, I became painfully aware of just how strenuous our three-day hike was going to be.

While stumbling down the mountainside I reviewed the little I knew about opium, most of which amounted to romantic myth. I had read *The Quiet American* by Graham Greene, and I pictured delicate Phuong preparing Fowler's evening indulgence while sinful Saigon throbbed outside their apartment. Another book I had read, *Junkie* by William Burroughs, conjured up stark images of strung-out addicts prowling the back alleys and ghettos of America's inner cities. But I had never stopped to consider how the spy and the heroin addict were connected.

From my work as a photojournalist I knew the military was concerned about rising drug abuse on its bases at home. I knew the problem was attributed to Vietnam veterans, but I didn't know that it was our government's allies in Laos and Thailand who grew the opium that was processed into the heroin that was sold to American soldiers in Southeast Asia.

I wasn't completely to blame for my ignorance. The fact that the CIA was managing the opium trade, in order to finance its Secret Army, was not being reported in *The New York Times*. Like most Americans, I had no idea that the CIA was even fighting a secret war in Laos. Again it was not a story that was appearing in the *Times*. But my naiveté was quickly vanishing and as we descended into the Montagnard village, I began to get a sense of what was really going on in that remote part of the world.

We arrived an hour after daybreak. We knew we were nearing the village when we passed through a series of small dikes diverting water from a stream. The water was being fed into little gardens, but the gardens were barren and the water was for cooking, not for irrigation. Clearly the villagers depended almost totally on food flown in by their American sponsors.

As we drew nearer we could smell morning meals being prepared and we could see little wisps of smoke through the trees. Then the forest receded into a partially cleared area consisting of raised huts interspersed among a few shade trees that had been left standing. Built hastily on the side of the mountain, with a minimum of effort, the huts were made of bamboo and did not appear to be permanent dwellings.

Hunters and fisherman as well as warriors, the Sedang, when left alone, are self-sufficient and rarely make contact with the outside world. Hence what is normal for them is somewhat shocking for the average middle class American. Pigs, chickens, goats and dogs roamed freely in between and under the raised thatched huts, and the placed reeked of dung. But the decrepit old men and women, and dirty children, were friendly and accepting. They offered us food and water (which we declined in favor of our own) while they affectionately welcomed their men folk—our guides and bearers.

To my surprise the village included half a dozen Americans dressed in camo fatigues, frayed boonie hats, green T-shirts, and an assortment of Sedang accessories, including necklaces, bracelets, and rings. Their hair and beards were getting long, so we knew they'd been there for several weeks at least. The American soldiers, who were undoubtedly with the US Army Special Forces, were heavily armed and had the look of wild animals. Then again, who else but a wild man would volunteer for such a job?

The Americans had their own compound on one side of the village, which we were steered clear of for the obvious reason that our presence constituted a threat to their good standing in the community, should trouble follow in our wake. We had not been allowed to stay in the village the night before because uninitiated strangers bring bad luck to the Sedang, and the same suspicious sentiment was evident among the Green Berets, who viewed us warily from a distance as we were ushered quickly passed their compound. Only the Major was allowed inside to pay his respects and confirm any arrangements that had been made in advance. As we were led to the northern fringe of the village we could see radio antennae protruding from their hut. We also saw a medic in front of the hut treating several Montagnards for the various ailments (malaria, dysentery, tuberculosis, and vitamin deficiencies, just to name a few) that plague primitive people living in unsanitary conditions. Plants and roots, sorcerers in touch with the spirit world, and ritual sacrifices were the only other remedies available to them.

Although the medic was sincerely trying to help the Sedang, I got the feeling that his show of dispensing medicine was a charade staged for our benefit. The main objective of the Sneaky Petes was not humanitarian; it was directing the soldiers on top of the hill. In any event their mission had nothing to do with ours, so we remained as inconspicuous as possible, maintaining the delicate balance between fact and fiction.

Having obtained the necessary clearances for our safe passage, the Major emerged from the American compound and we left the village. It was foggy when we departed and I felt like a character in a Jules Verne novel embarking on a voyage back in time. As we stepped off the edge of civilization—if one can call a Sedang village civilization—the sense of high adventure was visceral, exhilarating.

To the west lay a cloud-covered valley separating us from a parallel range of rugged hills, barely visible through the overcast sky. If all went well in another day we would be across the valley, up the opposite hills, and on the plateau.

*   *   *

That first day we moved quickly north along the ridge. In some places the vegetation was thick, but in others the terrain was more like a plain; the side of the hill was dotted with tall trees and the ground underfoot was grassy. It was the end of the dry season and the skies were cloudy, the air heavy with humidity, and there was a feeling of imminent rain. Some of the scenery was spectacular and at one point we saw a beautiful waterfall tumbling into a swift stream. It looked inviting but time was of the essence. In fact our first break wasn't until noon, and I got the impression that the Major was pushing us extra hard just to put some distance between us and the village. We circled up in a grassy spot under some trees, then the Team Leader sent Dil and Davy to scout ahead. He also sent two people back down the trail to make sure we weren't being followed. Everyone was on high alert, but grateful for a chance to rest and eat. Our lunch came in freeze-dried pouches. There were no campfires or conversations.

After Dil and Davy returned we formed up and moved out again, stopping every two hours to catch our breath, take a piss, and have a drink of water. At no time could I see the entire length of the patrol, which was broken up into three groups. But from what I could see, the security people had done this sort of thing before. Like the Montagnards they never wasted a move.

The final stop came at 6:30pm, just before dusk, about twelve kilometers from where we began. The route had been plotted in advance I believe, and we stopped on a ridge where people obviously had camped before. The ground rose to it and fell away from it, and there were medium sized boulders and fallen tree trunks providing cover and a field of fire. Again the Team Leader circled us up to form a defensive perimeter, sent out scouts and posted sentries. For the first time that day we were told we could remove our packs and draw the items we would need overnight.

Rusty and I were assigned a position next to each other, and we sagged down with our backs against a log. People were moving around and Rusty took the opportunity to whisper into my ear. "Not so bad so far, huh?" He was putting on a brave face.

I nodded my agreement. It wasn't the hardest hike I'd ever been on.

As darkness gathered around us the Team Leader brought us our ration of pre-packaged, high protein food. He also issued a stern warning. "Don't move outside the perimeter," he said. "We've set Claymores and trip wires all around. If you've got to take a piss, scoop a hole, flip it out, and roll on your side." He also told us to apply some more insect repellent and check our weapons before it got dark. He told us to make sure the safeties were on, but to keep them close in case we needed them.

The Team Leader slipped away and we poured the unappetizing contents of the packages into our cups, mixing it together with water from our canteens. Unless you enjoyed highly salted, flavorless food served at room temperature, the meal was satisfying only to the extent that it filled our stomachs and replenished our strength. The fortified protein bar was my favorite.

After supper the bustling stopped and throughout the night the Montagnards and security people took turns on watch. We technicians were exempted from that chore due to our inexperience and unreliability. We had also been split into pairs, with José and Taurus positioned across the campsite from Rusty and me. There was not supposed to be any chatter, but the darkness and evening chill added to our apprehension, and we couldn't help commiserating.

"I'm worried," Rusty said dejectedly under his breath. "I'm really scared."

"I know what you mean," I replied. "If I'd wanted to get my balls shot off, I would have joined the Marines. But it's too late to turn back now. We've just got to see this thing through."

We were wrapped in our ponchos, propped against our rucksacks in half-sitting positions, and I could tell from Rusty's anxious breathing that my words had done little to allay his fears. I realized that I was beginning to think and talk, like the Major, in hollow platitudes. Had I accepted too much?

The only noise that night was an occasional muffled cough coming from one of the nearby Montagnards. I wondered if he was afraid and figured he probably was, but not about the things that frightened Americans. No, the Yards believe their souls leave their bodies at night while they sleep and wander aimlessly around the forest. Their biggest fear is that their souls will get lost and not return to their bodies before they awake.

Pretty crazy, huh? Until you realize that tigers once roamed this remote part of the world, and that everything the Montagnards know about world history was told to them by their grandparents. So they believe in the Emung, the mythological tiger that creeps up silently and devours people in the middle of the night. There is no defense against the Emung, not like there is against human predators. It's simply a matter of fate.

Ask yourself, is their fear any less rationale than ours? Aren't we all preyed upon by our ignorance?

Before I fell asleep, Atlas crept over and whispered into my ear. "Hey buddy, the NVA coming down the Trail like to surround little camps like this at night. They wait for the first guy to sit up in the morning, then let him have it before they waste the rest of the team. So whatever you do, don't be the first asshole to sit up tomorrow morning. Sweet dreams," he said as he faded away.

And with that encouraging thought I tried to get to sleep.

*   *   *

Drifting fog engulfed the campsite when we awoke on Day Two. Our ponchos were wet with dew and though it had yet to warm up I was already feeling strung out. Sleep had come in fitful intervals, but in my state of semi-consciousness I made sure I wasn't the first jerk to sit up, just in case Atlas wasn't bullshitting me.

Breakfast, cold and bland, was consumed in silence as the forest came to life. We answered nature's call, reapplied our camo paint, refilled our canteens, took malaria pills, and formed up fast. The Team Leader told us that the enemy patrolled the valley below, and that contact with other people was to be avoided at all costs. For that reason we would be using an infrequently used trail. The going would be much harder and slower than usual, but it was better than running into an ambush. Stay alert and be quiet, he reminded us, and with that we were off.

Within half an hour the foliage was getting thicker and the heat and humidity were climbing higher, and by the time we hit the floor of the valley the ground was swampy and soggy, and it stank. Suddenly I missed the open spaces of the highlands.

Being in the first group didn't help either. I could no longer see anyone from the second group, let alone the third; but I could see Davy and Dil up ahead, sniffing around like bloodhounds for telltale signs (like broken branches or footprints) of people; for booby traps like Punji sticks and Malayan whips; and for avenues of escape. Behind them the Major and the Team Leader were setting an unusually slow pace and were calling for frequent breaks, during which they would check their compasses and maps and confer with Dil. At times it seemed like they might have lost their bearings, which added to the mental strain of knowing there was an armed and deadly enemy nearby. I kept thinking of how easily we could be bushwacked down here. More than anything else I wanted them to hurry up and get to the other side of the valley, so we could get the mission over with.

The worst part of the day was at mid-morning. We were floundering in a swampy area and may have been lost. There was a lengthy discussion during which it was decided to make up for lost time, and perhaps grease our skid into oblivion in the process, by stepping onto a more frequently traveled, parallel trail.

The word was passed down the line from mouth to ear: "In case of abrupt enemy attack, head for the right flank or the rear."

One part of me was terrified but another was glad. The valley was dark and gloomy and full of strange sounds and shadows that only added to my fear. Human instinct drives a person toward open spaces and light, but at the same time, why rush headlong at the enemy?

In any event, the decision was made. After a short rest and something to eat we moved diagonally through the forest, stepping cautiously onto a well-traveled trail. For safety's sake Pring and Klun were positioned as "flankers" on either side of our column, and Sammy and Song started walking backwards at the rear of the column, just in case we were over taken by a smaller, faster patrol behind us.

Even on the open trail it was tough going. The ground was anything but level, and was covered with tangled roots and loose rocks. But we were finally moving along at a steady pace in the right direction, and even if we were risking our lives, it was better than being lost.

Indeed the afternoon of Day Two proved to be pretty exciting. Whenever we crossed a perpendicular trail, we would first step off the one we were on, move parallel for about fifty feet, then jump across at a safe distance from where the perpendicular trail intersected ours. While the rest of the patrol crossed over, our flankers would watch up and down the perpendicular trail from concealed positions visible only to the Team Leader, who was directing traffic.

It was right after noon when the first incident occurred. Dil, Davy, and the Major had already crossed over when Klun, the flanker to the north, signaled that an enemy patrol was approaching fast! There was a moment of panic when, as fate would have it, I was just about to step into the open. Everyone was motioned to Get Down and Take Cover! Fortunately the four people who had gone before me had left no footprints—a feat I know I could not have accomplished.

I was hiding behind a tree and from my position on the edge of the trail I watched in abject horror as a patrol of about a dozen heavily armed men passed in front of me heading south on a high-speed trail bisecting ours. The first man was a Pathet Lao guide wearing a purplish uniform and a rakish white scarf made from pieces of a torn US Air Force parachute. The rest were dressed in the khaki uniforms of the NVA and were carrying AK-47s.

For the first time in my life I felt the urge to kill. But I held it in check.

The object of our mission was to get in and out unseen, so we let them pass, even though they had made a big mistake that should have cost them their lives. The first rule of any patrol is: "If you make time, you make noise," and they were making both. If they had been more alert, and if they had noticed us, we would have had no choice but to blow them away. But it was their lucky day.

The other exciting event of Day Two was our passage, late in the afternoon, through a village that appeared to have been bombed and evacuated a long time ago. Song, who was very brave and had scars on both shoulders from bullet wounds, entered the village alone to snatch some potatoes from an old garden. His Sedang tribesmen were delighted with the treat and ate the potatoes with little leaves they plucked from various bushes and shrubs. I later learned that the Montagnards are fastidious about their bowel movements, and believe regularity is a sign of spiritual well being. The roughage kept them on an even keel so to speak, and even though it slowed us down a little, the Major and the Team Leader felt it was worth the wait.

Beyond the ghost town we crossed a wide stream then began our ascent up the far side of the valley. Up ahead Dil and Davy searched for a safe place where we could rest over night, and they eventually chose a bamboo grove about two-thirds of the way up the steep three thousand foot hill. Dusk was rapidly approaching and there was a brief discussion in which the Team Leader persuaded the Major not to press on to the top. The patrol was exhausted he said, and considering our close encounter with the enemy patrol, the security people would be getting little sleep. The Major deferred to the Team Leader's judgment and once again the Team Leader set us up in a defensive perimeter, posted guards, and had the security people set up Claymore mines and trip wires.

The Major wanted to know if we should dig in, but the Team Leader said it would take too much work and that it was better to let us rest. We would need our strength tomorrow, in order to compensate for the time we had lost today.

By then darkness had fallen and there was no time to do anything but check our weapons, eat, and curl up in our ponchos. Everyone was in a high state of alert. There was no protective cover where we were and a confrontation would have spelled disaster, so no one spoke or moved about. We all just sat there praying to God that the passing patrol, or someone hidden in the ghost town, hadn't seen us.

Once again sleep came fitfully, if at all.

Chapter Eight

During the 1966 Christmas bombings of North Vietnam, the NVA moved thousands of troops into the Mu Gia Pass for infiltration down the Laotian Corridor into Cambodia and South Vietnam. Guided by their Pathet Lao and Montagnard allies, the NVA patrols traveled by day in units as small as six men, and at night on bicycles and in camouflaged trucks in battalion-sized outfits having as many as six hundred men. At times the NVA even risked transporting troops in flat-bottomed boats down the Kong River, which scribed the eastern boundary of the Bolovens Plateau. But more often they chose to travel through the sparsely populated valleys to the west, proselytizing to one another at night in sanctuaries and supply centers hidden in huge caves in the hills.

The objective of American Recon Teams in Laos was to pinpoint the number and location of NVA troops and trucks along the Ho Chi Minh Trail, and report this information back to headquarters so the US Air Force at Nakhon Phanom, Thailand (where the 56th Air Commandos were based, and where our C-130 probably landed after dropping us off) could launch bombing attacks against confirmed targets. This deadly game of cat and mouse had been in progress for over five years by the time we joined in the fun, and the evidence was everywhere.

On Day One we had traveled north for about twelve kilometers along a ridge in the hills, and on Day Two we had cut across the valley, but had gained only five or six kilometers and had fallen behind schedule. We had a specific amount of distance to cover in a finite amount of time and meeting our appointment—not safety—was the Major's primary goal on Day Three.

The professional soldiers in our group were certainly aware of our predicament, but they didn't show any concern, and with only an inkling of the true extent of the danger we were in, we rose before dawn on Day Three and prepared to crest the hill.

We had consumed the water and food carried by two bearers, which gave us two extra Montagnards to act as armed escorts, and that was encouraging. The bravery and loyalty of the Sedang was no longer in doubt, and having taken the sacred oath with the Major, it was their sacred duty to protect him, and us, with their lives. As they knelt at the base of the bamboo trees, digging up tasty young shoots for their breakfast, I found yet another reason to admire them.

At sunrise we started up the hill. It was a steep climb and at times we were on our hands and knees. Half an hour later, with the sun beginning to shine on our backs, we reached the western edge of the Golf Course. Breathing a collective sigh of relief we gazed back across the valley at the ridge we had traversed two days before. It was a clear day and the ridge looked impossibly far away.

As we formed up in single file, the Team Leader outlined his plan for the day. He said the hardest part was behind us, but that we had lost some time and would have to move fast to reach our objective on schedule. The trail would be wider, the terrain less difficult, but we would have to be on high alert for enemy patrols and—a new factor in the equation—activity in the air. At the first sound of approaching aircraft, even if the plane appeared to be American or South Vietnamese, we were to immediately take cover. "If anyone sees you out here," the Team Leader warned, "they'll blast you off the face of the earth, then inquire about your nationality."

With that we took off fast heading west over gently rolling hills, the type that can best be described as a tropical savannah, with fields of tall grass, swamps, and groves. A cool breeze made breathing easier than the day before, and the temperature was tolerable.

The advantages of the new terrain brought new risks however, for now we were exposed. In open areas I could see the entire length of the patrol stretching out behind us, and the lack of cover quickly became our chief concern. Not fifteen minutes had elapsed from the moment we began moving across the plateau, when we heard the drone of engines and the unmistakable sound of rotor blades; a few seconds later we saw our first helicopter of the day. Everyone ducked for cover on either side of the trail as a Huey, flying north, passed behind us at an altitude of about one thousand feet. The chopper did not have American markings and was probably piloted by South Vietnamese. The word came down the line that it was "running the ridge."

Four or five more times that morning we spotted unmarked Hueys flying north and south behind us, and even though they grew further and further away, we had to dive for cover and wait until they disappeared. Each interruption slowed our progress of course, and during Day Three we did not stop once for a break.

To some degree we were becoming careless. The mission had achieved a momentum of its own, a sense of urgency that propelled us forward and made enthusiasts of us all.

The Major seemed totally unconcerned about ambushes and he pushed us harder than before, despite the fact that there were trails crossing ours. There were, however, no villages in this blasted No-Man's land.

At noon we passed the burnt out wreckage of an F-105 fighter. No sign of the crew remained, and a demolition team had blown up the plane. The entire area had been heavily bombed and some of the craters had formed into little pools of muddy brown water. But the most curious incident of the day occurred when a fixed wing propeller driven aircraft appeared in the early afternoon. It was a two-seater, and was moving incredibly slowly at about fifteen hundred feet. Definitely foreign manufactured, it was unlike any plane I'd ever seen before.

By mid-afternoon we were closing in on our objective and by late afternoon we had covered more than ten kilometers from the rim of the plateau. We were now in a heavily forested area. The Major called a halt in a small clearing and while Dil and Davy scouted ahead, the Team Leader told us to prepare our evening meal. But no one was hungry. Although winded and tired we were coiled too tight with anticipation. The moment we were waiting for was about to arrive.

Speaking confidently, animatedly, the Major said to everyone: "We've closed to within two kilometers of our objective. It's a large enemy encampment and even though they're not expecting anyone from this direction, there are sure to be some sentries along the trails heading in. But they're on their own turf, and we're not expecting them to be prepared." He looked around. "We're almost back on schedule, so we can slow down the pace to minimize noise. Our only advantages are surprise and stealth, so we have to tread very lightly from here on in. Is that clear?"

Everyone nodded that it was.

"Good," the Major said.

We had been moving into the setting sun, and from where the trail emerged from the trees, Davy and Dil signaled that all was clear ahead. While the shadows grew longer and the darkness gradually engulfed our little group, we formed up and moved out in single file, proceeding for one and a half clicks, at which point the Major called another halt. Night had fallen completely as we circled up and formed a defensive perimeter. The darkness slowed us down but our eyes were adjusting to it, and knowing we were half a click away from an enemy encampment had our hearts beating fast, despite our fatigue. We were told to remove our rucksacks and prepare our cameras, which I did, attaching one lens to each camera body, loading each camera with film, attaching one camera to a special snap on my pistol belt and then snapping the other camera to a special harness that was crisscrossed over one shoulder, across my chest, and belted to my waist. This way the cameras were secure and would not jostle around and make any unnecessary noises.

The remainders of our supplies were distributed, with each man getting one day's ration of pre-packaged food and two canteens of water for the return trip. The bearers with the ammo stacked their packs in the center of the clearing and everyone but we technicians filled the empty pouches in his BAR belt with M16 magazines. Rusty, Taurus, José and I would be going in without our rifles, because we would need to have our hands free to operate our camera and sound equipment. We did, however, fill our ammo belts with as many nine-millimeter slugs as we could.

Meanwhile the security people were doing their thing. Atlas was checking his M60 and directing the Yards who were carrying his extra belts into positions near him. Sammy the M-79 grenadier was loading up his OD pouch with grenades. The Team Leader, Davy, Reb, and Joey had removed all their gear, reapplied their camo paint, and tied black bandanas around their heads. The handles and blades of their Gerber Mark IV daggers were black so as not to reflect any moonlight. They made ready their black nylon garrotes, and the tiny four-inch crossbows with the four-inch long, poison tipped arrows—silent, instant death from fifteen feet.

Dil and Song were smiling as they crept passed me to join the Team Leader. As Dil passed me, he muttered the only English words he knew: "Eat Lao soul."

Doc handed Dexedrine pills to the Team Leader, Davy, Reb and Joey. Leaving their equipment and weapons behind, except for their pistols, Gerbers, garrotes, and crossbows, the four Rangers joined Dil and Song and moved down the trail, their knees bent and their fingertips nearly touching the ground.

After they had vanished Doc moved among us, handing out Dexedrine pills and telling us to take some now and put the rest in our pill kits for later on, if and when we needed the boost. My adrenaline was pumping so fast I could not imagine that need arising.

About twenty minutes later the four Rangers and two Montagnards came creeping back into camp and conferred with the Major. They were stained with blood and they did not have to announce that the wet work had been completed. They had cleared away any potential problems, had a feel for the terrain, and had made visual contact with the enemy encampment. "We can go in now," the Team Leader said with conviction.

Knowing the security people had murdered in cold blood had a sobering effect. Now we could expect the same, even worse, if something went wrong. But everything was going as planned and the Major had everything under control, so even though everyone was very uptight, no one was freezing. We all knew one thing—the sooner we got the mission over with, the sooner we could get the hell away.

The Team Leader brought Rusty, José, Taurus and me together with Reb, Joey, and the Major for our final briefing. Speaking very softly, the Major said: "We're going to deploy into three groups. I want each of you to photograph and record what you see from as many different angles as you can, so we can really get a picture of what's happening out there. The idea is to keep moving and not stay in one place too long. Understand?"

We all nodded yes.

"Remember," the Major continued, "We're looking at this encampment as a trafficking point for opium, and we'd like you to get as much detail in that respect as possible. So whenever you can, focus on the opium." He looked at each of us individually, his thin lips drawing back in a semi-sneer, the anger he felt in his heart spilling over into his voice. "But," and he said the following words with real animosity, as if we were all guilty by association, "we're also here to find out if there are any Americans involved in what's going on. And if there are Americans involved, we want you to take their pictures and record their words. Understood?"

We understood. Perfectly.

"Okay," the Major said, addressing himself to the security people. "We'll be heading out in three groups. First is you," he said, pointing at Joey. "You take him (Song), him (Davy), him with the wide angle lenses (Rusty, who looked skinnier and younger than ever before), and him (one of the Montagnard bearers). You five will move out first, heading west along the southern perimeter of the encampment, then edging north to get pictures of the action from that side. Got it?"

Joey got it.

"Then get ready to go.

"Second group. That's me and you Chief, and him (Dil), him with the zoom lenses (me), him with the sound equipment (José), and him (another Montagnard bearer). The six of us will move along the southern perimeter, going in behind the first group, only slower and in closer, taking photos and sound recordings from that angle, which will be the closest to the action.

"Third group. You'll be leaving after Group Two. That's you," the Major said, indicating Reb. "Take the M-79 with you, him (Pring), those two (Montagnard bearers) and him, the man with the video," meaning Taurus, who was weary from the hike and having a hard time keeping up. Taurus had taken an upper and it seemed to be making him more jittery than alert. "Group Three will reconnoiter the eastern edge, as far north and as in close as possible. Remember to keep moving and not to stay in one place too long. Okay?"

Reb acknowledged that everything was okay.

"For the time being," the Major said quietly, "everyone leaves his rucksack and extra gear here. Photographers, just take your cameras, pistols, and a canteen. Doc and the gunner (meaning Atlas) will stay here with them (pointing to Klun and the two remaining bearers) to cover our rear and keep an eye on the gear. We'll rendezvous here just as soon as all the film is expended. Not before."

He took a breath, the excitement quickening even his rock steady pulse. "No matter what happens, we get the film back to Jason."

What he meant, of course, was that the film came first, people second. He was placing a higher value on several rolls of silver-oxide coated plastic, than on the lives of twenty-two human beings, his own included.

The Major then issued one last set of instructions. "Tomorrow afternoon we'll be extracted by helicopter from a hill top on the ridge, approximately twelve kilometers east-north-east of here. Be there or be square."

He wasn't joking, and he turned his attention to the four security people. "The photographers and the soundman are your responsibility. If any of you get separated from the rest of us, follow one of the two trails drawn in black to the coordinates marked in black on these maps." He handed a mini-map to each of them. "Do not follow the trails marked in red, and do not go near the coordinates marked in red. Got it?"

They got it, knowing the trails drawn in red were decoys in case one of them was captured or killed, and the map fell into enemy hands. They put the folded maps in their breast pockets.

"That's it," the Major said flatly. "First group, get going."

CHAPTER NINE

It was so dark I could barely see, and it was hot, although the heat I was feeling was generated more from within than without. I wiped the sweating palms of my hands on my pants and took a salt pill, hoping that would help.

Don't get me wrong. My immediate concern wasn't the danger anymore; it was how to get the job done. I felt this was a once-in-a-lifetime opportunity to prove myself and to accomplish more, as part of a precision machine, than I could ever accomplish alone. Sure, the other parts had lied to us, but they were just doing their job and they had gotten us this far in one piece. Now it was our turn to deliver the goods. We had to get in close, photograph the place and the people, then get away unseen.

Up until now everything had gone pretty much according to plan and I truly believed we could pull the mission off without any problems. My big concern was the unfavorable conditions. I had to contend with humidity, darkness, mosquitoes attacking in force, tangled underbrush, and the fact that my hands were trembling and my knees were weak. These were hardly optimum conditions for photography. But the Major had brought me to my apotheosis, and I was determined to play my part.

Then it was time to go. The first group had gone five minutes before and the third group would go five minutes later. We were strung out in single file: Dil at the point, the Team Leader, the Major, myself, José and the other Montagnard. We moved as quickly and boldly as possible up the gradually rising terrain, which flattened out when it reached a thickly forested ridge running east and west. We began walking west, weaving our way between the trees and shrubs, catching our first whiff of the sickly sweet smell of opium. I thought I could hear voices.

It was then that I realized how lucky we had been. There was no way we could have taken decent photographs in the rain. But the sky was clear, the stars were twinkling, and a three quarter moon was rising from behind the pinnacle of a mountain in the north.

For those few moments I felt like we were fated to succeed. I felt a sense of relief, too, knowing the end was in sight and that our escape route was mapped out.

My automatic was snug in its holster on my left hip, within easy reach, and the camera with the 500mm lens was on my right hip attached to the belt on my harness. The camera with the 200mm lens and the starlight scope was securely fastened where the straps of the harness crisscrossed in the center of my chest. I was anxious to put the equipment to use. I was ready and raring to go. The only thing bothering me was the profound sense of isolation. I felt like the first man on the moon.

Veering north, crouching low to the ground, we crept slowly toward the edge of the ridge where it dipped down into a grassy ravine. Three feet from the tree line we stopped, knelt, and parted the underbrush. The vegetation was thick and provided us with excellent cover, and when we poked through we saw, less than a hundred yards away, a small town divided by a narrow street with a dozen huts on either side. Firelight emanated from the open-faced huts on the south side of the street, illuminating the contours of the thatched huts lining the north. At the eastern edge of the encampment, disappearing into the distant dark shadows, was a vast field.

Without having to be told I unsnapped the camera on my chest and brought it to my eye, knowing the 200mm lens would let me get more of what I saw in the picture frame. And the first thing I saw was the source of the light: inside each of the open-faced huts was a roaring fire blazing beneath a cast iron pot, pungent smoke swirling away in every direction on the shifting wind. And they weren't cooking Irish stew. They were boiling opium, then pressing it into bricks the size of gold bars.

A Chinese chemist and a team of Chinese assistants were managing the processing and the pressing, which was being done by Lao Theung workers. Lao Theung workers also wrapped, carried, and stacked the opium bricks in a heavily guarded storage hut at the western end of the encampment. Everybody was thoroughly engaged in his labor and none of the guards seemed overly concerned; it was as if they had been anesthetized by the pungent fumes of the powerful narcotic.

It was vital that I get a closer look so I unfastened the camera with the 500mm lens from the harness on my hip and snapped the camera with the 200mm lens back in its place, switching the starlight scope in the process, all of which took twenty seconds. With the image intensifier attached I could see more clearly than anyone else in my group, and because the huts had their sides rolled up for ventilation, I was able to photograph everything that was happening. We could not have arrived at a more auspicious time.

Camera buffs might be interested to know that my shutter speed never changed, but stayed permanently set at one-sixtieth of a second. Because there was more starlight than expected, I did adjust the size of the lens opening from F4 to F5/6. A larger F-stop means a smaller lens opening, and a smaller lens opening means less light is required to properly expose the file, resulting in a sharper picture. And with the F-stop set at F5/6, I knew I was getting some fantastically clear pictures. But best of all, the camera didn't make a sound.

*   *   *

During the course of the next forty-five minutes we changed location four or five times, carefully backing away from the tree line, then moving west behind the cover of the trees and shrubs along the ridge. Each time we inched in our formation remained the same: the Team Leader watched our left flank, Dil the right, while the Major placed himself between me and José, so he could ask questions and make suggestions about what I was photographing. José had yet to start recording.

The ridge curved north as we moved further west, eventually arriving at a point where we could see an airstrip at the western edge of the encampment, about fifty yards from our position. Just as we reached that point we heard the sound of an approaching aircraft. It was a few minutes before eleven. Excitedly, the Major motioned for us to drop back and move laterally north and west along the ridge onto a promontory which was as close to the airstrip as we could get. As I mentioned above, José had not been recording up until then and as we slid into position, the Major told him to prepare himself.

"The buyers are about to arrive," he whispered. "Concentrate your equipment on the area between the airstrip and the storage hut."

As the plane above prepared to land, a contingent of workers from the opium compound was sent to ignite torches and hold them aloft on both sides of the makeshift runway. "Be sure to get photographs of the aircraft once it's on the ground," the Major said eagerly, as the Lao Theung torch-bearers moved into place.

The scene unfolding on that desolate plateau was spellbinding, almost festive, as the torch-bearers formed two wavering parallel lines, and the people in the huts stopped what they were doing and looked to see. Those who weren't doing anything drifted west in a throng, listening to the throb of the engines in the night and then gasping as the outline of the plane's undercarriage materialized in the glow of the hand-held torches, its wing tips passing mere feet from the bearers. A muffled cheer went up when the plane touched down, and as it rumbled to a southern edge of the runway the torches were extinguished and an expectant hush fell over the crowd.

The Major was nearly jumping out of his skin. Speaking as loudly as he dared he said: "Get as many pictures of the people as you can." Then turning to José he said, "And you, get every word they say down on tape."

José dutifully armed his dish while the pilot turned the aircraft around so it was facing north, ready for immediate take-off. We could see it perfectly; a vintage, wide-bodied, twin engine, silver colored DC-3 with no markings. I half expected Terry and the Pirates to disembark. But this was no cartoon and when the cockpit door opened two older men—one white, the other black—climbed down and began inspecting the plane's undercarriage and landing gear. Four younger men armed with Uzis emerged from the cargo hatch at the rear of the plane; two stayed in the plane, the others got out and stood beside their bosses.

The pilot was a thickset man in his mid-forty's, dressed in a black aviators jumpsuit. His co-pilot was an imposing black man about six feet four inches tall, in his mid-thirties, with bushy muttonchop whiskers and a bushy moustache. He was wearing a tan Abercrombie and Fitch safari jacket with pockets everywhere and a shoulder holster strapped outside it. Inside the holster was a .38 police special. While I photographed the black man I tried to decide if he was a pure Afro-American. Something about him made him appear Moroccan or Asian, but I couldn't tell for sure. He was wearing a Rolex watch and a nice gold ring and was sweating profusely under his stylish outfit. I was impressed.

The Major, however, nearly lost control when he saw the two older men. Even at that distance he was able to recognize them. He was crouched behind me and José and I felt his hand on my shoulder. "Get those two faces on film," he commanded.

With the 500mm already in my hands I was able to do just that. A face did not fill an entire frame, but I was close enough to fill a frame with a body from the chest up.

Meanwhile a group of workers had wheeled out several fifty-five gallon drums filled with aviation fuel. They also had hand pumps and what looked like garden hoses. As they began to refuel the plane the Major leaned over to José. "Tell me what they're saying," he said, then added angrily, "We ought to blow them away right now."

I could feel his breath on the nape of my neck but by then, nothing was turning my attention away from the job at hand. I let the sweat trickle down my face and I let the mosquitoes drink their full. I felt calm and in control.

I was shooting as fast as I could, using the 500mm lens to get detailed shots of each individual. These pictures would easily allow Mr. Jason's people to positively identify the two senior CIA agents, the four mercenaries who composed their security squad, the opium lord and his lieutenants, and the Chinese chemist and his staff. In a darkroom under an enlarger every mole, scar, whisker, and wrinkle on each man's face would be visible. By changing the focus on the 500mm I also got full-length photos that would provide other types of clues. And when I wanted a shot of the plane with everyone assembled in front of it, which is where the deal was going down, I switched back to the 200mm. I had about three hundred shots coming to me and I wanted to use them all.

Some things I still remember very clearly. For example, the four mercenaries were dressed alike but not in any style of clothing I had ever seen before or since. Their shirts were loose fitting like flak jackets with sleeves, and their pants were loose fitting like fatigues, but were a shiny metallic silver color. If I had to take a guess, I'd say the mercenaries were ex-servicemen who had done a tour or two in Southeast Asia, then become ex-patriots and were now making big bucks in the drug business while working their way up the corporate underworld ladder.

The two older men, who were conducting negotiations with the opium bandits, were very interesting. The black man in particular. He had tiny tufts of curly black hair above and behind each ear, and was balding on top. His hooked nose and thin lips looked more Indian than Negroid, and his bushy eyebrows seemed clownish above his eyes. The older white man had a receding hairline and small features, but his most distinguishing feature was the fact that he was missing two fingers on his left hand.

While I was capturing the action on film, José was zeroing in on their conversation with his mini-dish, simultaneously recording it on tape and relaying what he heard in hushed tones to the Major. "They're making the deal," he said. "They want to buy five tons of opium from these guys."

"They're talking to the seller," he continued. "The five tons was agreed upon prior to tonight, but they're dickering over the price. There's no-pre-arranged price. The sellers want sixty dollars per kilogram; the spade's offering forty. They're at an impasse. The spade and the pilot are conferring, and now the spade says he wants to taste it."

At that point the opium lord turned to one of his men, who passed the order down to a minion. A crate was chosen at random from among the many that were to be loaded into the plane. The crate was pried open with a crowbar, a brick of opium was unwrapped and a sliver was sliced off. The sample worked its way back up the chain of command to the opium lord, who handed it to the black man, who pulled a pipe and two test tubes from one of his Abercrombie and Fitch pockets. Rolling a piece of the opium into a tiny ball between his fingers, he expertly filled the pipe. Everyone watched in anticipation while he flicked open a cigarette lighter and put the flame under the bowl. The heat caused the opium to blister and when he put the stem of the pipe in his mouth, I could see that one of his front teeth had a unique, star-shaped gold filling. He drew a deep breath, then slowly exhaled a stream of smoke. His reaction was muted as he rolled another piece of opium into a ball, dropped it into a test tube, and poured a chemical solution from another test tube into it. The results of the experiment pleased him and there were smiles and nods of approval all around.

The pilot and co-pilot seemed relaxed, but the four young mercenaries were very uptight. They had flipped the safeties off their Uzis, and they kept vigilant watch on the opium bandits' security squad. But there wasn't any cause for alarm. Although the opium bandits greatly outnumbered the Americans, they seemed to be negotiating in good faith. They had, however, crowded closer to the scene of the transaction, forming a semi-circle near the cargo door of the DC-3. It seemed like the mercenaries were posturing to keep them back.

Once the quality of the opium had been ascertained, the conversation resumed and José began talking again. "The older white man is offering fifty dollars per," he said. "That's his final offer, and the sellers are accepting. They've settled, and now they want to see the cash."

At that point one of the mercenaries in the plane handed down a portable scale and a sizable strongbox, which were placed side by side on the ground. The older white man tossed a key to one of the mercenaries who unlocked the box. Inside were stacks and stacks of Yankee greenbacks. Determining the denominations would have to wait until the film was developed, but at fifty dollars per kilogram, the price of five tons of opium had to approach a quarter of a million dollars.

It was breathtaking to see that much cash in one place at one time. My eyes were glued to it, as were the eyes of everyone else in the compound—except the mercenaries. They were scanning the crowd for any sign of trouble. There was no guarantee that some third party wouldn't try to steal the loot.

If only they knew.

Next a group of workers began carrying the crates filled with opium bricks over to the plane. Each crate of opium weighed about a hundred pounds, minus the uniform weight of the crate, and each crate was placed on the scale and weighed while the two CIA agents and the opium bandits watched. The black man had a pad in his hand, as did the opium lord's lieutenant, and each made a notation as the crates were weighed and handed up to the mercenary in the plane. The plane must have been stripped inside and I wondered if the DC-3, which was at least twenty-five years old, could even get off the ground. But they kept on weighing and loading and by the time they were done I had used up all the film in the camera with the 500mm lens. Only a few shots in the 200mm remained.

The process of weighing and loading was time consuming, but nearly one hundred crates were accounted for by midnight. No money had changed hands, however, and only when the plane was fully loaded did they make the exchange. The black man and the opium lord's accountant did some final tallying, and the throng of people began to stir restlessly while they waited for the payoff.

Two of the mercenaries were standing astride the strongbox while the other two watched from the cargo door. José told the Major, "Our guy says his figures show four thousand five hundred kilograms. At fifty per, that's two hundred twenty-five thousand dollars. Their guy agrees. Our guy says there's a quarter of a million in the box and he's gonna take out the difference. That's twenty-five grand."

When the black CIA agent was finished removing the surplus, which he stuffed in his pockets, the opium lord's accountant bent down and counted the rest. "He's satisfied it's all there," José said. "The deal's done."

My last pictures captured that poignant moment. I also got a few shots of the opium lord's assistants grabbing the strongbox and taking it to his hut. The Chinese chemist would get his share, which he would invest wisely in legitimate businesses. The opium lord would buy some guns, but most of his money would go into a numbered bank account in Switzerland.*

The plane was refueled, filled with raw opium, revving and ready for takeoff. Having made a fortune, the opium bandits were in a jubilant mood. Our business too had been successfully concluded and I felt pretty good as I snapped my cameras in place. José packed away his mini-dish and headset and we waited for the word to withdraw.

Then, rising over the noise of the airplane and originating from the area to our northwest, came the riveting sound of gunfire. The mad scramble for survival had begun.

---

* In 1975 General Vang Pao paid $200,000 cash for a four hundred acre farm in Missoula, Montana.

Chapter Ten

Seconds after the gunshots announced our presence the entire encampment erupted in pandemonium. Guns were popping and people were yelling and scrambling around, and the black CIA agent was closing the cockpit door while the DC-3 rumbled down the runway, picked up speed, then climbed into the obscurity of the midnight sky.

The people in the camp paid it no heed. In their rush to locate the intruders they were scurrying frantically in all directions at once, bumping into one another and shouting confused and contradictory commands. There were sporadic bursts of automatic weapons fire as panicked sentries blasted at shadows and mirages moving on the periphery of the camp. Finally one of the cooler heads ordered a worker to hand crank the generator that powered the search light atop the old French lookout tower. Pointed toward the northwest corner of camp, it slowly began to sweep in our general direction. It was time to go.

Surveying the scene the Major said very calmly, "Don't shoot back. They don't know we're here and we don't want to draw their fire." He was worried about the first group, however, and was weighing the risks of going to help them out, waiting for them, or leaving without them. His better judgment prevailed and he muttered irritably after a few seconds, "Let's get the hell out of here."

Gingerly we backed away from our vantage point on the promontory. The bushes and branches closed behind us like a door, and we didn't bother covering our tracks. Exercising as much restraint as possible, we followed Dil east along the ridge in single file staying south of the noise, smell, and glow of the enemy encampment. The probing searchlight fell on our vacated position moments later, its wide beam penetrating less than a foot into the forest before it dissolved in the thick vegetation. Bullets accompanied the light—reconnaissance by fire, it's called—clipping the bushes where we had been a moment before. But nothing came close to our formation and within a minute we were out of range and safely on our way to the rendezvous.

The temporary state of chaos caused by the opium bandits having been caught off guard gave us the grace period we need to reach the little clearing in the woods where we had stacked our weapons and equipment. The third team was already there and had fortified the defensive perimeter established by Atlas, Doc, and the two Montagnards. While the rest of us had been spying on the opium bandits, they had rigged mechanical ambushes in strategic places approaching the clearing, and Atlas had set himself up behind a log with a Yard and extra ammo belts on either side. The area was sufficiently secure to reduce the terror that held me in its grip.

At the Team Leader's instructions José and I grabbed our M16s and filled our BAR pouches with at least ten magazines each. We made sure our canteens were filled and that we had ration packets. As those preparations were being completed the five excited members of Group One emerged from the darkness. They'd slipped away unseen without returning fire and without anyone getting hurt. As far as they knew they hadn't been followed either; but as everyone knew, it was only a matter of moments before we would be discovered.

That being the situation and everyone being assembled, the Major began issuing commands. "Photographers, ditch all of your excess gear. Keep your film and tapes, and that's all."

We did exactly what he said. We popped the film from our cameras and the cassettes from the audio and video recorders, and then stashed the evidence in custom-made waterproof canisters in pouches on our pistol belts. We ditched the cameras, recorders, mini-dish and carrying cases off the trail. Then we waited, nearly jumping out of our skin.

"It's midnight now," the Major noted. "That gives you sixteen hours to reach the hilltop where the choppers will pick you up at sixteen hundred hours. The tightrope walk is over. From here on out it's a foot race and you gotta travel light to travel fast." He paused to listen and have a look around, and then said, "Carry your weapons, ammo, water, food, and film. You'll need the radio too, but that's it."

Believe me when I say I was itching to go. But the Major was not about to be rushed. His voice was stern but he was calm, as if he had been planning for this moment all along. I remembered his ominous words when he showed us Mr. Jason's picture.

"Now I want you in two groups," he said. "First group takes the southern trail marked in black. That's you, Numbers Two and Three (meaning Reb and Joey). Take those two," pointing at José and Taurus, "plus Klun and those two (bearers). Now scram."

The seven of them formed up and took off down the trail at a trot.

"Chief," the Major continued. "Take the second team along the north trail. That's everybody but me, Dil, the gunner, and the two Yards with him. We'll be staying here to cover you. Get together quick and didi beaucoup."

Then slipping into Montagnard, the Major spoke to Dil. Both of them moved into position near Atlas, who had listened with cool indifference while the Major pronounced his death sentence.

I was standing in that little clearing, paralyzed in place. The others were already up and moving but I was trapped between my feelings of pity for Atlas, and my seething hatred for the Major. It didn't matter to me that *he* was staying behind; I despised him anyway. "You lied, you bastard," I thought to myself. "You said this mission was going to be safe! So stay behind and cover my ass, motherfucker." As if reading my thoughts the Major glanced over his shoulder at me. The expression on his face was haughty, aristocratic.

The Team Leader grabbed my shoulder and spun me around. "You got one second to decide if you're coming with us," he hissed. His knife was in his hand.

I never looked back. My instincts for self-preservation prevailed. Though the injustice made me sick to my stomach, I took off with the Team Leader knowing that Atlas, like the other security people, had volunteered for the mission knowing it might come to this. It was something I understood at that moment, but still cannot explain.

Intermittent gunfire had come from the opium camp during the ten minutes we stood in the clearing and organized our departure. Next there had been a lull, which meant the bandits had regained control of their forces and that search parties were scouring the area for tracks. It was only a matter of how long before they stumbled into the ambush laid by Atlas, the Major, and the courageous Montagnards.

Ten minutes was the answer. We were ten minutes and a thousand yards away when all hell broke loose in that little clearing in the woods. The first sounds were those of Claymore mines being detonated and ripping apart the bodies of the opium bandits who had stumbled upon them. The Major had sprung his trap and for the next ten minutes we listened to the boom of the M60 intermingling with the longer bursts of M16s and the blasts of exploding grenades. At one point the staccato sounds were so sustained as to resemble a single protracted clap of thunder. But night ambushes quickly spin out of control and after the initial contact, when the opium bandits took their highest casualties, the ambushers themselves became the focus of concentrated fire. What had begun as a full-scale war gradually evolved into a skirmish in which the positions of the combatants were constantly changing, and single shots were all we heard. By the time we were thirty minutes and half a kilometer away there was only silence.

The significance of the silence was not something that has to be explained; everyone knew the Major and Atlas and the three Montagnards had been surrounded and picked-off, one by one, and that those who had not been killed outright had been wounded and captured, which meant torture and a slower more painful death. All five had given their lives so we might escape; emphasis on might. And yet due to the nature of our "secret" mission, no one would ever know or pay homage to their beau geste. It's that sort of senseless loss that gnaws at the gut of every soldier who fought in Southeast Asia. Whether or not you liked them as individuals, it's a bitter thought that so many young men died without any recognition for their sacrifices.

Sentimentality aside, those of us who remained alive had no intentions of holding a memorial service. The security people in particular still had a job to do, and that job was to get the film back to Jason. Their attention was focused fully on the task at hand.

Having been graced with a thirty-minute head start, they were confident we could outrun our pursuers. The security people and the Montagnards knew exactly where we were and exactly where we were going, and even though it was the middle of the night and deep in the jungle they unanimously agreed we could reach the designated coordinates at the appointed hour, but only if we kept on moving.

Pring was at the point. Following him were the Team Leader, Davy, me, a Yard, Rusty, Sammy the M-79 grenadier, and Song bringing up the rear. The ground underfoot was solid, the trail relatively clear, and we were gearing our pace to our own physical limitations; which considering the exertion, lack of sleep, and stress of the last few days were rapidly diminishing. No one was even thinking properly so periodically we stopped to catch our breath, check our points of reference, and listen for unusual sounds. I could barely hear anything above the howl of my aching muscles, but each time the Team Leader told us to stand and start moving I responded. When you're running for your life you tend to find the hidden reserves.

For the next three hours we proceeded in twenty-five minute bursts, stopping for five minute breaks then tunneling again into the darkness, our strength sapped, our legs as heavy as lead, our lungs burning, our brains numbed by fear and fatigue. Each step was becoming a supreme test of will power, an immense effort based only on the belief that it carried us further from harm. But there was as much danger ahead as behind and somewhere around 3:00am we collided with an enemy patrol. We never knew if they were coming to get us or if they were as surprised as we were. Not that it mattered. The physical exertion had taken its toll and we weren't as alert as we should have been, and they got the drop on us. The only thing we saw were muzzle flashes up ahead coming right at us, less than thirty feet away.

Pring went down immediately with several gunshot wounds in his chest, the impact lifting him onto his toes and knocking him backwards onto the ground. The Team Leader dove right, Davy left, and I went the same way as the Chief. Behind me I heard Sammy scream, "Lord have mercy!"

I landed five feet behind the Team Leader and the two of us buried ourselves in the dirt as a volley of bullets whizzed overhead. Neither of us was hit.

"How far ahead are they?" Doc yelled from behind a tree, intentionally trying to draw their fire. A hail of bullets answered his query.

The next thing I knew the Team Leader was crouching on his fingertips and toes. He put one finger to his lips then turned the palm of his hand down, indicating that me and Sammy, who had crawled to within five feet of us, should stay put. He moved off to his right, intending to outflank the people who had pinned us down.

Attempting to draw their fire again, Doc yelled, "Ho Chi Minh sucks dick!" But the fish weren't biting, so Sammy kneeled and let loose a buckshot round at the place where the muzzle flashes had been. Two AK-47s erupted from slightly to the left. Our security people knew where the enemy soldiers were hiding, and they knew there weren't many of them. For their part the enemy soldiers knew we were trying to draw their fire and outflank them, but they weren't fast enough.

Two bursts of M-16 fire came from the left, one from the right, as Davy, Song, and the Team Leader converged. Nothing happened after that for a few seconds, and then we heard footsteps coming down the trail and the Team Leader saying, "Hold your fire." Davy and Song were turned completely around, backing down the trail behind him.

"Two are dead," the Team Leader said, "but one got away." Looking around anxiously he asked, "How bad are we hurt?"

"Pring bit the big one," Doc said grimly. He was bent over the body examining two sucking chest wounds. Pring was on his back unconscious but not yet dead. Gurgling noises came from his throat and I could smell the blood. "There ain't nothing I can do for him," Doc said matter-of-factly.

We stood in a group watching him die and wondering what to do. I'd seen him get hit and when he fell back, I'd seen his look of stunned surprise. I'd never seen anyone get shot and killed before, and I felt sick.

The Team Leader turned away in frustration. "Put him out of his misery, Doc," he said between clenched teeth. "We can't wait around."

"Not necessary," came the response. "He's gone."

Running his hand over his head, the Team Leader asked irritably, "Anyone else get hit?"

"Over here," Rusty groaned, walking forward. He was gripping his left arm just below his shoulder, and when Doc turned him around you could see that he'd been shot clean through. Sweat poured from Rusty's forehead and he was obviously in pain.

Doc quickly examined the wound, then announced that a small caliber bullet had passed clean through without hitting any bones. But for some reason—more likely shock than self-control—Rusty had managed to lie still and keep his mouth shut during the ambush. Not knowing what else to do, he sat down.

"Shit!" the Team Leader mumbled as Doc dressed the wound in the darkness, and then gave Rusty a shot for infection. He gave him a little shot of morphine for the pain too, but not enough to immobilize him. Rusty was going to have to grin and bear it.

Squatting down beside him, the Team Leader asked: "Can you make it?"

"Hell, yes," came Rusty's indignant reply, as Doc helped him to his feet. "How else am I gonna get the hell out of here," he said a little unsteadily.

While Rusty hobbled around to prove he was okay, Sammy made the point: "We can't go on like this. We need some rest."

Biting his lower lip the Team Leader agreed. "Yeah, but what about that fucker who got away?" Having said that, he discussed the dilemma with Song, who evidently agreed that we needed rest. Song's reaction was not what the Team Leader wanted to hear, we could tell by his grimaces.

"So what's the verdict, Chief?" Sammy asked.

"Song doesn't like it. He says the NVA will be coming for us in the morning. But he don't see where we got any other choice. Neither do I. We gotta stay cool. We can rest for about two hours and still make it on time. We'll move down the trail a few hundred yards then duck off to the side and rest awhile. Let's get going."

We carried Pring's body out of sight, then the Team Leader formed us up with Song at the point, followed by himself, Davy, a Yard, me, Rusty, Doc, the other Yard, and Sammy. Nobody knew where the other team was. After what had just happened it seemed pointless to worry about them.

Chapter Eleven

As we moved off the trail that night into the bowels of the jungle, the fear of being cornered and captured escalated into stark, unadulterated terror. To guide us we had Song's unerring instincts and the Team Leader's tiny compass dangling from a string around his neck. But we had lost a lot of our confidence, and then it started to rain.

The downpour lasted only for about fifteen minutes, but to this day I can't sleep through a rainy night without dreaming that I'm back in that pitch-black quagmire of mud and clawing vegetation. Although we moved at a crawl, at times it was impossible to see the man next to you, so we constantly touched each other so as not to get separated.

After fifteen minutes of our wallowing around, the rain let up and we stumbled to a halt in total exhaustion; and after determining that we were all present and accounted for, the Team Leader said we would stay put until first light. Everyone was to try to get some rest except him and Song, who were going to take turns on guard. The rest of us munched some crackers and chocolate and drank some water. We also scratched at the insects that had crawled under our soaking wet clothes. Rusty's face, like mine, was bleeding from scratches and bites, and his eyes were red and filled with tears. I could see that he had reached his limit and I tried to find some words of comfort. They seemed to help. It also helped that neither of us had taken any Dexedrine, and despite our terror and depression, we were so tired we were able to get some sleep.

The sun had risen when I awoke a little over two hours later. It was after six o'clock. The security people and Song were studying the Team Leader's acetate terrain map and discussing our predicament. From what I overheard, we had traveled more than four kilometers from the opium compound and had a little less than eight to go to reach the extraction point. There was no time to waste, however. Doc put a new dressing on Rusty's wound, we checked our weapons, drank, ate, pissed and this time we all swallowed some Dexedrine pills. Then we moved.

It took us less than five minutes to reach the trail and the first thing Song said to the Team Leader—who interpreted for our benefit—was that a Pathet Lao patrol had passed a mere fifteen minutes before, heading west toward the opium compound.

With those chilling words the apprehension swelled up in my chest once again. The Dexedrine was starting to kick in; it was making my heart pound and I remember looking at Rusty's bloodshot eyes. He looked like a wild man, but I could tell he was ready to go and for some reason that calmed me down. The feelings of panic have never quite subsided, but that morning I was reconciled to the probability that unfriendly people would be waiting for us somewhere along the way. We didn't know what we would be running into but we had to make a run for it. We were eager to force the situation to its climax and to end the uncertainty once and for all.

We were a ragged looking bunch, quite the worse for wear, drenched and filthy with cuts and welts on our unshaven faces, and our eyes red and swollen from lack of sleep and the effects of amphetamine. But we weren't dead yet. In fact, we were energized by desperation and the slim chance we might make it out.

The nine of us formed up as usual and started moving. The terrain was fairly level, the trail high-speed, and soon the trees and shrubs on either side began to thin out as we gained the plateau. Our passage was as swift and silent as possible with brave Song far out in front. No one was talking or lagging not even Rusty. We were a runaway train ready to roll over anything that got in its path.

There wasn't any other choice. There was only one way out, we had just under eight hours to get there, and for the first four hours we flew, taking only two quick breaks at two hour intervals and covering half the distance to our destination by noon.

Notably, we did not attempt to make radio contact until our second break at noon, for the simple reason that we didn't want to let the enemy pinpoint our location. If they were listening and if they intercepted our transmissions, they could probably figure out where we were heading. In any case Doc's radio had an FM line of sight and was useless in the jungle unless a plane was directly overhead. But by noon we were on the plateau and it was the right time to stop, eat, catch our breath, check our points of reference, and call in. The idea was to get through to the original base camp on the mountain top, which we could see in the distance, so they could alert the Forward Air Controller back in South Vietnam to get some choppers into the sky above us. The FAC would then direct the gunships and slicks that were to rescue us.

While Doc put in the call the Team Leader sent Song up the trail and around a bend to keep watch. It was a lucky thing he did. Doc had made contact, our message had been relayed, and just as the Team Leader was saying, "Head 'em up," Song came scurrying down the trail giving the clenched fist signal that people were coming in our direction.

"Let's kill the bastards while we got the chance," the Team Leader said.

"What about ammo?" Doc inquired.

"No! Get 'em now," came the frantic response. "Everyone off to the right. Wait for my signal," the Team Leader commanded.

Following his instructions we quickly faded into the cover of the trees and rocks on the right side of the trail, so we wouldn't get caught in our own crossfire. We flicked off our safeties in the process. There really wasn't much cover and as I hid behind a tree, the tension I felt was intense. I realized how lucky we were to have taken the break when we did, or else we would have run into another on-coming force, like last night. And if that had happened, some of us would have died for sure. It seemed like an omen; but for a simple twist of fate it could have been us walking into a trap.

My next thought was about what we were going to do to the enemy.

I looked at Rusty. He was half-lying on the ground, his right shoulder pressed against a tree, and he was squinting sideways through the corners of his bulging eyes. The bandage on his left shoulder was blood soaked and his left arm was in a loose sling. His jaw jutted forward. His lips were pale and stretched tight, barring his teeth. Every muscle in the face was taut giving him a haggard, sanguinary look. When you're close to violent death it's not so hard to kill.

How much he'd changed, I thought…watching…waiting.

We could hear the soft tread of people approaching then passing by in quick succession. It all happened very quickly and when the last man was abreast of his position, the Team Leader rose to his feet, the rest of us doing likewise. It was a point blank massacre. Once we were standing we had a clear line of fire at our enemies. The noise was ear splitting. Six went down immediately, two managed to spin around and shoot from the hip, but we blew them away before they could take aim. Their bullets thudded into the ground harmlessly.

We had caught them all in the first burst before they could scramble into the trees. The slaughter was so complete there was no need to examine the corpses. We'd killed them all. For a moment the only sound was the metallic clanking of fresh magazines being shoved into M16s. The smell of cordite and the stench of death mingled in the air. The enemy soldiers were wearing black pajamas and sandals, and were carrying machetes and rice bags on their belts. "VC in Laos," the Team Leader said in amazement.

"Coming to get us?" Sammy asked.

"Who the fuck knows," came the educated reply.

The only thing we knew was that they'd made a big mistake. Perhaps it was over-confidence. We knew we wouldn't be this fortunate again.

A single shot rang out in the distance.

"Holy shit!" Doc exclaimed. "That's less than a click away!"

"We gotta get outta here, now," the Team Leader said.

"What's going on?" I asked.

"Means we're being tracked," came the straightforward response. "It's a call signal. If they'd got the drop on us, these dead gooks would've answered with a single shot, or maybe two." He thought about it for a moment, grabbed an AK-47 and fired two rounds. Worth a try," he quipped, and then told everyone to take the last of his uppers.

While we gulped the last of our Dexedrine, the Team Leader conferred with Song. The Yard laughed savagely. "Song says the gooks can run all day," he chuckled. "He says we should boogie."

Wasting no further time on explanations, the Team Leader had us flick our safeties back on, form up and move out. Like hit and run drivers fleeing the scene of the crime we spun away from the ambush, never thinking about the carnage we had wrought, just making good our escape. We had four hours to cover just under four clicks and everyone for miles around knew where we were and what direction were heading in. That was the situation in a nutshell. And even though four kilometers may not sound like a hell of a lot of distance, under the circumstances it seemed like a voyage to the moon.

The speed kicked in and helped to compensate for the lack of sleep. But our bodies were drained of fluids and the dehydration was causing our muscles to cramp and our breath to come harder. The temperature was climbing as the afternoon sun began to beat down on us: by 2:00pm we were swooning and stopping every five hundred yards for a rest and drink. My one remaining canteen was less than a quarter full.

By 3:15pm I was on the brink of collapse and so was everyone else. But we had closed without incident to within half a kilometer of the hilltop Landing Zone we were to be extracted from, and it was finally time to call in the choppers. Using the code-name Quail to identify our patrol, and not forgetting to mention that the area was crawling with enemy soldiers, Doc called in our coordinates to the Forward Air Controller who was flying at fifteen hundred feet in a Cessna 0-2 several miles to the east. Doc confirmed that we could reach the LZ on schedule, gave its coordinates, and then waited for a response.

A smile spread across his face. Helicopter gunships and slicks were already on station warming their engines and planning their estimated time of arrival to coincide with ours. We downed the last of our water and tossed away our empty canteens. We were so close.

Song was pacing up and down the trail like a caged tiger, casting furtive glances in both directions and sniffing the air. The cocky Montagnard usually wore a frown, but now he had a devilish grin on his face. We had really raised some hell over the last twenty-four hours, the type of action that would live forever in Montagnard legend.

After returning from Sammy's position at the rear of the formation, Song spoke to the Team Leader, who passed the message back down the formation. "NVA coming up fast from behind. Be here in less than five minutes."

How he knew it no one knew. But no one doubted it was true.

Sammy looked long down the trail and slipped a buckshot round in his pirate pistol. Davy nodded his head knowingly and repeated the letters, "N. V. A." I think it was the first time I had heard him speak.

Doc depressed the antenna on his radio, stood up and declared, "I got a good copy, Chief. The choppers are airborne. The good guys are on the way!"

"Then let's get the fuck out of here," the Team Leader replied, shifting one of the other Yards to the point and having Song drop back to the rear where he felt his expertise was better served. I recall being so afraid at that moment, that just as Song was passing me on his way down the formation, I unconsciously switched my safety from On to Off. Smiling sardonically, the Montagnard scout stopped and switched it back On, indicating that I should stay cool.

We took off resolutely toward the LZ, more concerned about what was behind us than what was ahead. And that was our next mistake because three hundred yards down the trail we got hit. The Yard at the point, a young boy who may have been on his first patrol, got zapped right between the eyes. He never knew what hit him. The Team Leader and Davy reacted instantly, jumping off the trail to either side. But I stopped to think, "Oh, no! We're not going to make it!" And in that instant the sniper's next shot grazed my forearm, gouging out a chunk of flesh and bringing me to my senses. I dove to the right, feeling like I'd been stung by a giant bee.

No one else was hit, but we were pinned down again, this time no doubt by an NVA scout who had circled in front while we were making radio contact. The guy peppered us with automatic rifle fire.

Davy and Doc were side-by-side on the opposite side of the trail from where the Team Leader and I were hunkered down. Motioning to Davy, then looking at my arm and seeing it was just a flesh wound, the Team Leader signaled that it would be the same routine as before, then he slipped off into the underbrush while Davy did the same.

Song, Rusty, Sammy, and the other Montagnard watched our rear while Doc and I exchanged fire with the sniper ahead. The guy was on a suicide mission to slow us down, and a minute later there was a shoot-out forty or fifty meters ahead. Seconds after that we heard the Team Leader frantically yelling for Doc and me to come forward *fast*. He and Davy had taken out the bushwacker, but in the process Davy had been drilled through the thigh. The wound was bleeding profusely but Davy, God bless him, was determined to make it. We were just a few hundred meters from the LZ and the trail was cleared for us to move ahead.

Suddenly shots were coming at us from behind!

Using a black bandana, Doc tied a tourniquet around Davy's leg at the pressure point near the crotch, then we each draped one of Davy's arms over a shoulder and began helping him up the hill. After several steps, however, Davy shrugged me off, saying, "Go back and help the others. Doc can help me. You go back."

While Doc and Davy limped briskly along the trail, the Team Leader ran ahead to check out the LZ, and I fell back to the rear of the formation where a squad of NVA soldiers were snapping at our heels. I couldn't see any of them, but shots were coming at us and we were shooting back.

Under Sammy's direction we started leapfrogging down the trail. There were five of us—me, Rusty, Sammy, Song and the last Montagnard—with four men laying down fire while the last man ran to the head of the formation, ducked off the trail and started putting down cover while the next man retreated. Sometimes we were actually walking backwards while shooting, then turning around and running like mad.

This went on for five minutes, five harrowing minutes that seemed like forever, but in the course of doing this we were able to determine that there were only six or seven people behind us; enough for us to handle if our ammunition held out. But Sammy was running low on buckshot rounds, so making a virtue out of necessity, when he was the last man in line he let loose a gas grenade, reloaded and quickly fired another, creating a temporary smoke screen. With that we all dashed down the trail, reaching the bottom of a hill just as the Team Leader reached the same spot coming down from the other direction.

The six of us met at a point where the trail broke out of the forest into low bushes and scrubby trees at the base of a small, moderately inclined hill. We could see Doc and Davy struggling in tandem toward the top along a washed out, rocky streambed.

Taking a gulp of air to slow his heartbeat, the Team Leader gasped between breaths: "I've been to the top...three hundred meters away. Perfect. Level. Been cleared, but only room for one chopper at a time."

Gathering his strength he gestured for Song and the other Yard to stay with him at the base of the hill. He waved the rest of us up. We did what he wanted.

"Don't forget," he panted, looking at me. "Get the film to Jason."

A few minutes later we had over-taken Doc and Davy, who was sprawled on the ground less than fifty meters from the crest of the hill. Davy's mouth was wide open and his eyeballs had rolled back inside his head. Doc was yelling in the radio that we needed the choppers "ASAP! And protection too!"

Sammy and Rusty hefted Davy and began carrying him toward the top of the hill. Sammy was walking backwards with Davy's head against his chest and Davy's arms under his armpits. Rusty was hugging Davy's legs under his good arm. They were moving very slowly.

Down at the bottom of the hill there was a pitched battle going on and that made me think that more NVA had arrived on the scene. Automatics were cracking, grenades exploding. Meanwhile Doc had finished calling in and Sammy was screaming from above, "Get up here where there's cover! Get up here fast!"

"Fuck that," Doc cursed. "I'm going back for the Chief."

"Me too," I blurted.

Doc glared at me. "Hell you are, boy. You're getting that film to the top."

Just then the Team Leader (who had lost his M16) and Song came scrambling up the washout on their hands and knees, legs pumping like pistons, loose rocks and gravel churning up behind them. The Chief stumbled, Song picked him up, and they were off and running again.

Doc swung into action, lobbing fragmentation grenades over their heads. The Team Leader collapsed beside me muttering angrily that one of his own grenades had killed the other Yard; then he puked. Song stood over him using his body as a shield, blasting away with his M16. Sitting with our backs against the side of the hill, Doc and I each emptied a clip down the washout.

Raising his head and unholstering his Browning semi-automatic, the Team Leader said wearily, "They're probably re-grouping. Now's our chance. Let's go!"

With that the four of us lurched up the hill, turning at intervals and laying down a withering fire along the smoke-filled washout. I was the first to reach the summit and as I dropped down behind a log, I saw the Team Leader wheel around and holler, "Get down!" In the same instant he fired a round from his Browning at a dazed NVA soldier standing not five feet from Song. The bullet knocked the khaki-clad guy back down the hill. While the Team Leader, Song and Doc joined me behind the protection of the log, I zapped two more NVA soldiers emerging from the washout.

The top of the hill was covered with rippling waves of yellow-brown grass, a few low bushes, and some fallen trees. Sammy, Rusty, and Davy (who was unconscious) were staked out behind a log on the north side of the hill taking fire from an adjacent hill to the north about a thousand yards away. The three or four people standing on the hill were out of accurate range, but they had clear shots. The Team Leader called our attention to them and without thinking I squeezed off a shot and saw one of them go down. It was pure luck, but I felt exhilarated as they scrambled for cover themselves. "Fuck you, motherfucker," I yelled, then squeezed off two more rounds.

"Doc," the Team Leader said excitedly. "Get on the box! Get a gunship over there on the north!"

Two seconds later Doc was doing just that. Then he directed the second of the gunships that was circling overhead to blast the washout. Three slicks were circling over the valley to our east, waiting for the signal to descend. One gunship was blasting the ridge to the north, the other was swooping down along the washout, raking up as many NVA as possible.

Thinking the gravest danger came from the west along the washout, the Team Leader sent Doc over to Davy on the north, with instructions to send Sammy back to him; and just as Sammy was halfway to us, two NVA soldiers crested the hill beside him. They were on their hands and knees and barely had time to look up when the Team Leader shouted at Sammy, "To your right!"

The startled NVA looked at the Chief while Sammy dropped to one knee and fired an explosive round into one man's chest. Song stood up and took out the second one with a burst of his M16. As he stood there smiling a bullet from an AK-47 knocked his frayed boonie hat off his head. Song dropped back down beside me still grinning from ear to ear, as Sammy slid into Doc's vacated spot.

In the meantime Doc had made it safely to the position on the north, while the gunship suppressed the fire that had been coming from the adjacent hill. But the gunship buzzing the washout had veered away and an NVA squad was advancing up the hill. The Team Leader rolled his last willy peter (white phosphorous) grenade down the slope; there was an explosion and a huge pillar of smoke spread skyward. People below us screamed and a grass fire started burning on the side of the hill, the wind pushing it toward us, raising even more smoke than before, blocking our view.

We heard Doc screaming, "South! To the south!"

Coming over that side of the hill, hunched over and scrambling for their lives, were José and Klun. The other team had made it!

Pointing at me the Team Leader said, "Get over there and give them some cover!"

Instantly I was on my feet and running and as I dropped down beside the log where José and Klun had positioned themselves, I saw what looked like an entire company of NVA soldiers slowly advancing up the southern slope of the hill.

Everything started to happen at once. Joey came over the crest of the hill about thirty feet to our east and took a bullet in the back about an inch above his waist. His mouth dropped open as he slumped to his knees, sighed, then rolled over on his side. In a second Reb and a Yard were dragging him behind a log and signaling to Doc for help from above. The gunship that had been employed on the north joined the spotter plane in shooting up the south side of the hill, while the other gunship began running the washout on the west. The NVA were closing on three sides. On the east was a cliff.

José was beside me blasting away with his M16 and when he paused to shove in another magazine I asked him, "Where's Taurus?"

"We've been waiting down there for an hour. When you guys showed up, so did the NVA." His wide wild eyes sent mine the unspeakable message of murder. "Taurus was lagging coming up the hill. He took a bullet in the back." José gasped. "Then that fucking homicidal maniac from the South put a bullet in his head and gave his tapes to me."

José crossed himself and mumbled a prayer. Then he tapped his ammo belt where he had his audiotapes and Taurus's videocassettes.

Just then the Cessna 0-2 joined the fight. It had under-wing pylons equipped with 20mm mini-guns and rockets, and it came swooping in low, chewing up the ground *ten feet* in front of us! The NVA were that close! Fragments of earth, wood and rock whizzed over the log behind which José, Klun and I were hiding. I counted about twenty small explosions as the Team Leader popped a red smoke grenade and yelled, to my surprise, "Get the wounded out first!"

Doc and Rusty lifted Davy and headed for the first of the unmarked slicks coming in. Reb and a Yard were carrying Joey through the prop blast. The spotter plane and one gunship were blasting away on the south, the other on the west. I told José to get going and he did. And just as he left I emptied a magazine and reached for another…and found none! I didn't know what to do! Klun and I were alone on the south side and I desperately felt the need for more firepower than my Browning. Klun motioned for me to get down: two NVA were emerging from the smoke less than ten feet in front of us.

The first slick was taking off with Rusty, Davy, Reb, Joey, José and a Yard. Doc had scrambled back to his position on the north. The slick had risen fifty feet straight up into the clear blue sky then dipped down and banked toward the east over the valley, when a three man NVA squad appeared at the spot where Joey had gotten hit, and blew it out of the sky with a Russian-made, rocket propelled grenade launcher.

I couldn't believe it! The chopper exploded in a huge orange ball then dropped out of sight behind the brush-covered cliff, like a meteor.

Sammy came charging across the hill from the west, shrieking like a banshee, stopped, stood thirty feet from the RPG squad and put an explosive round right on top of them. Body parts flew everywhere and the blast started another fire. Sammy threw himself on the ground, reloaded, stood up and raced over to our position.

Meanwhile Klun had sprung to his feet and shot the two NVA soldiers who were about to take cover on the other side of *our* log. Klun jumped over, stripped them of their AK-47s and ammo belts, and leaped back. He handed me an AK and two clips, showed me how to load it, and smiled as he pointed at my pants where I had pissed in them. The gunship and spotter had made a pass, and once again the remnants of the NVA were advancing up the hill. Klun and I started blasting away with our AK-47s.

Over on the north side of the hill Doc was directing two F-4 Phantom jets, which were dropping ordnance all over the west and south sides of the hill. Napalm. Five hundred pound bombs. Everything!

Sammy was standing and cheering, "It's the Air Force! It's the fucking Air Force!"

With the arrival of the Fast Fours there was a lull in the sharp stutter of AK-47 fire coming at us. The Team Leader popped another red smoke and the second unmarked slick came in. Grass was burning on three sides of the hill. Clouds of red, black, and white smoke swept over the top, fanned by the chopper blades. Six NVA broke from cover at the place where Sammy had obliterated the RPG squad. Klun and I killed three and the rest hit the dirt. Sammy laid his last explosive round on them, then turned and raced toward the hovering slick.

The world was unloading like an avalanche. All of us were converging on the chopper; Doc from the north, Song and the Team Leader from the west, Sammy and Klun and me from the south. As the others boarded, Klun and I turned and emptied our weapons then tossed them away.

The Phantoms were making another run. The gunships were nearby spitting bullets. The Cessna was circling above, directing the show. There were explosions, smoke, shots, fire, shouts!

The chopper swung around and as I stepped on the skids a bullet smacked into it about a foot from my head; as the chopper was pulling away, Klun and Sammy pulled me in. The door gunner, a black guy with a flak jacket but no patch on his shoulder, opened up over my head with a fifty caliber machine gun. Green and red tracers were coming at us from the west and there were holes in the hull of the chopper where some of the bullets were impacting. Doc, Song, and the Team Leader were sprawled on the floor, but no one inside was hurt.

"Do you see anyone!" the gunner yelled.

"Yeah, over there on the west," his assistant said.

The gunner cut loose as the Team Leader twisted himself around so he was sitting beside me.

"Claim a kill," the man feeding ammunition to the door gunner said.

"You think so?" the gunner said skeptically, gazing into the smoke as the chopper rapidly ascended.

"Oh, no question about it, man," the other guy said casually as the chopper banked toward the east, missing a gunship by about thirty feet. Everyone gasped.

Half a dozen NVA appeared on the top of the hill, in between the drifting clouds of smoke. They stood there and fired a volley, missing us completely. The Team Leader was leaning out of the slick squeezing off shots from his Browning as the hill faded away. The pistol was pointed down and smoke was curling up from the barrel. The door gunner laid his hand on the Team Leader's shoulder and said, "It's all over, man."

The Team Leader dropped the magazine from his handgun. It was empty.

Yelling over the roar of the engines, the door gunner's assistant asked me in a thick Southern accent, "Where you boys been?" He was grinning widely.

I was feeling everything so fast, I couldn't think of anything to say.

Chapter Twelve

The helicopter ride into South Vietnam remains a blur. All I can recall is sitting in the doorway with my feet on the skids, in a state of wonderment, thinking, "Thank God I'm alive."

Two hundred feet below, the green mountains slipped by as fast as the flood of feelings rushing through me, leaving me dumbstruck, in awe. I couldn't believe it was possible. But it had happened and my amazement was tempered only by the supreme joy I felt at having survived. It was over and I was alive!

I hadn't known them long, but the vividness and immediacy of the deaths of the other men only intensified my newfound awareness of the fragility and richness of life. Being alive was good. In fact, it was all that mattered. It was reward enough for everything that had transpired in the past few days. It was like a private joke I shared with the world, one that might have sent me into hilarious fits of laughter under other circumstances. Instead I sat there speechless, a disembodied spirit savoring that rare intimation of what it means to be immortal.

Then the chopper landed, the rotor wash creating fantastic winds, pelting everyone with dirt and debris. We were climbing out, people were approaching us, and Doc was muttering to no one in particular, "I could use about twenty-four beers."

"Me, too," Sammy said, then asked the Team Leader, "You coming, Chief?"

"I'll join you in a minute," he said.

Sammy put his hand on my shoulder and said, "Take care of that arm," then skipped off with Doc to find the nearest refrigerator.

"This thing ain't over for you yet," the Team Leader said to me. "You're not safe until Jason gets the film and hears what happened. The best way to protect yourself until then is to keep your mouth shut." He extended his hand. "You did good. Be cool."

I took his hand, wondering what I was going to do without him. Flanked by the mighty Montagnards, Klun and Song, our intrepid Team Leader cast a menacing "Keep your distance" look at the officers standing nearby, then shuffled off to his debriefing.

I never saw him or any of the others again, I think.

Beyond the rolls of barbed wire, upon which people's clothing was hanging, was a stretch of open land cleared by that notorious weed killer Agent Orange. Ragged hills surrounded the firebase we had landed at. There was a lookout tower, listening posts outside the perimeter wire, and three-man mortar and machine crews inside it. Everyone was wearing flak jackets and helmets with graffiti scribbled on them. I seem to remember it was the 173rd Airborne, perhaps at Dak To. But to this day I have no clear recollection where the firebase was, though it was obviously way out in Indian country.

One of the officers standing nearby led me to the command post beside the airstrip where the helicopter pad was located. The command post was a reinforced bunker built of sandbags, logs, and sheet metal. The few people loitering around it strained their necks to see what was happening. There were off-duty engineers, Vietnamese soldiers rolling bones in the shade by a prisoner compound, and a few curious men wearing Green Berets—one of whom would notify his CIA case officer at the local

Embassy House that something strange was going on. The message would be relayed in real time to the CIA's Security Chief in Saigon, and the red flag would be raised in every CIA compound in South Vietnam.

After a brief period of sitting around saying nothing, the officer told me it was time to go. As he hustled me into a newly arrived Huey, he motioned to another officer and said, "He'll be your escort as far as your destination."

Like I said before, I was crashing and I don't recall where I was, but within ten minutes of my arrival I was airborne for the second time that day. The sound inside a helicopter resembles a series of quick explosions, and unless you yell it's impossible to carry on a normal conversation, and I was too emotionally raw and too exhausted to make the effort, so I sat beside the escort officer, asking no questions, being asked no questions, and not giving a damn. We were cruising at about a hundred and fifteen knots, and only at the end of the trip did the mountains level off. Everywhere I looked vast sections of the countryside had been defoliated, and there were huge bomb craters that looked like inverted mushroom caps.

We were flying northeast I believe. The setting sun was behind us and it was dark when we arrived at the US Air Force Air Base in Danang. Waiting for me there was an armed guard of Air Force security people under the command of a lieutenant colonel wearing the red and yellow MACV (Military Assistance Command, Vietnam) patch with the sword in the middle. I distinctly remember that. The lieutenant colonel thanked the escort officer and watched while he walked away. Then he asked me, "Have you got the film?"

I said I did and he said, "Good. Now let's get your arm taken care of." At his direction the security people took me over to a dispensary where my wound was cleaned and stitched and bandaged. I was not allowed to shower, but I was given clean fatigues, and then led back to the lieutenant colonel's office. He posted two guards outside the room and told me to be seated.

The lieutenant colonel was tall and thin, in his thirties, with clear blue eyes. He had the look of an educated intelligent man…maybe an Ivy

Leaguer. He lit a cigarette, offered one to me, which I refused, then asked, "What happened out there?"

I was struggling to stay awake and was uncertain of my status, but I remembered what the Major had said ages and ages ago. "I'm sorry, sir," I replied respectfully, " I just don't know."

He was standing behind his desk, gently tapping the ash of the cigarette into an ashtray he picked up and carried around the desk. Sitting on the front edge of the desk, he leaned forward so we were face to face. Quietly he asked, "What were you shooting?"

My answer was direct and to the point. "With all due respect sir, you must know that I'm under orders not to say anything to anyone, except to a man whose face I'll recognize when I see him." Showing my resolve, I asked, "Do you know where he is?"

The light colonel took a deep drag on his cigarette, exhaled a stream of smoke, and said, "He's on his way. He'll be here soon."

I got the feeling his questions were a sort of test. He also seemed sympathetic, to the degree that any officer can sympathize with an enlisted man.

He said reassuringly, "Don't worry. I'm here to help. Is there anything you need?"

When I said I could use a little sleep he stood up, snuffed out his cigarette, opened the door and called in one of the security people. "Take this man to your billet and let him crash on one of your bunks so he can get a few hours sleep. God knows he can use it." Then he turned to me and said, "You look like Christ off the cross."

Addressing the security guard again, the droll lieutenant colonel said, "Keep this man under close watch. Don't let him out of your sight and don't let anyone touch him. I'll let you know when I want you to bring him back."

"Yes, sir," the security guard said, chuckling at the officer's irreverent wisecrack. But that was exactly how I felt: resurrected. So I was dismissed and went to the security guards' billet, which was large enough for a small platoon, and I got a few hours rest.

*   *   *

Just before midnight I was awoken and informed that the MACV lieutenant colonel wanted to see me immediately. I threw some cold water on my face and four Air Force security guards escorted me to his office. Upon arriving, three of the guards entered the room with me and one stayed outside. The atmosphere was relaxed. The light colonel said the person I was expecting had just landed and would be here any minute, and right after he said that there was a knock at the door. We could hear a commotion outside and suddenly the door flew open and three men in civilian clothes barged into the office, followed closely by the security guard. One of the younger men slammed the door behind him while the oldest of the bunch, a pint-sized, roly-poly balding man, flashed a badge that identified him as CIA.

The two younger CIA agents were carrying Swedish Ks, and the security people reacted instantly, pointing their shotguns at the chests of the intruders. The lieutenant colonel jumped to his feet, knocking his chair down. He demanded to know, "What's the meaning of this?"

From the tone of his voice I could tell he was intimidated. Every intelligence officer knew the CIA ran the Vietnam War from behind the scenes, and the lieutenant colonel was obviously surprised and uptight. The only sound was the hum of the air conditioner, but the room was crackling with tension.

The ranking CIA officer was livid. "Tell your men to lower their weapons," he demanded.

"What?" the lieutenant colonel exclaimed incredulously, knowing his career was hanging in the balance. His mouth was wide open.

Slipping his ID back in his pocket and then motioning toward me, the roly-poly CIA officer said, "We want that man."

I was half sitting, half standing in front of the lieutenant colonel's desk, when one of the younger CIA agents took a step toward me.

"Don't do it," the lieutenant colonel spat, his demeanor changing from passive to aggressive as he moved around his desk. "If he makes another move," he said to the guards, indicating the young CIA officer who was about to grab me, "shoot the son-of-a-bitch!"

"You got it sir," one of the security people said very coolly, before any of the CIA people could react, and that seemed to swing the advantage back to the colonel.

Outrage and fear were etched on the face of the young CIA officer standing in front of me, while the other one traded menacing glances with the security people. But when it came right down to it, the shotguns won.

The ranking CIA officer tried to rally his forces. "We want this guy. I'm warning you, colonel, don't interfere."

"Oh," the colonel replied in mock surprise, jerking his thumb toward me, "You want *him*." The CIA officer in the middle of the room took a step back and as he did that, the colonel walked up to the plump little CIA officer. Psychologically it was the coup de grace. "You want him," he said in the man's face, "then take him."

Not one of the CIA agents moved a muscle.

Smiling slightly, the light colonel, who had recovered his sense of humor, told his ranking security guard to disarm the spooks. The security guard passed the order along to his men, who grabbed the Swedish Ks and the CIA officers' handguns. Meanwhile more Air Force personnel had gathered in the hall outside, bolstering our forces.

"That's how it is with you sissies, isn't it," the lieutenant colonel sneered. "Not tough. Not good. Just arrogant." He nearly laughed in the face of the roly-poly CIA officer. "Now get the hell out of here and take your garbage with you, before you wind up in the cage."

In a last bitter attempt to save face, the ranking CIA officer vowed indignantly, "You'll never get away with this. You can kiss your career good-bye."

"Is that so?" the LTC replied as the security people pushed the younger CIA agents out the door. He knew everyone was watching, and that something bordering on the momentous was occurring, and he had decided, impetuously, to wave the flag.

"Well," he stated emphatically for the benefit of his audience, "in this compound, you're just three pieces of shit." He looked remarkably like Johnny Carson trying to keep a straight face after delivering one of his famous one-liners.

Well, that did it. That was the final insult. While the Air Force security people laughed in their faces, the CIA officers left in disgrace, the roly-poly one muttering hotly under his breath, "We'll be back."

But the good guys had won another round, and two minutes later Mr. Jason appeared at the door.

Chapter Thirteen

The Vietnam War taught America some hard lessons.

For the true believers, it was the supreme test and loss of faith in the ideal that all Americans are united in a common cause. For them it was a matter of, "My country, right or wrong," and they could not accept the fact that their fellow Americans would settle for anything less than total commitment, total victory. They felt betrayed and were wounded to the core of their beings when faced with the harsh reality.

Ironically, Vietnam veterans who learned to oppose the war (like myself) also felt betrayed. But we never felt betrayed by the citizens who opposed the war back home. We felt betrayed by the people who led us into it.

The difference is not the grief we feel. We all honor the soldiers who fought and died. The difference is as intangible as the spirit that moves us in different directions.

Consider Mr. Jason.

Mr. Jason was a frail looking older man dressed in plain green fatigues. He introduced himself, but did not produce any identification. That wasn't necessary, of course, as I immediately recognized him the moment he walked through the door.

The MACV lieutenant colonel asked if we wanted any coffee, which I accepted and Mr. Jason declined. After he returned with my coffee, the lieutenant colonel lingered outside with the security people for a few minutes, and then retired to his quarters. It was well after midnight.

Mr. Jason walked behind the lieutenant colonel's desk and placed his briefcase on it. He opened the briefcase and removed a miniature tape recorder and several blank tapes, one of which he inserted in the recorder. Next he removed a legal pad and a ballpoint pen, and then he sat down. He placed the machine on the edge of the desk facing me, pressed the Play and Record switches, and politely asked me to state my name, rank, and serial number. When I finished doing that he re-wound the tape, played it back, adjusted the volume, turned it on again, and asked, "Do you have something for me?"

Handing the film to him I said, "Yes, sir."

"Thank you," he replied, describing the film canisters as he placed them in the briefcase.

He was a mild-mannered man with thinning grey hair and light blue eyes. As I said before, he could have been anyone's grandfather. He looked into my eyes as if he were trying to see behind them, hesitated, and then asked me, "What happened to your commanding officer? Why isn't he here?"

"As far as I know sir, he was killed or captured."

"I see," Mr. Jason replied mechanically, masking his sadness. "What happened to the other photographers and the person making the audiotapes?"

"I was told that one of them was killed by gunfire, and I saw the other two go down with the chopper, sir. None of them made it out."

"I see. And you were not able to recover their film or tape?"

"No, sir," I said apologetically.

Pulling a white handkerchief from his back pocket, Mr. Jason wiped the lenses on his glasses and held them up to the light. Showing no emotion he said, "Tell me, please, what you saw and anything you might have heard while you were filming."

I remember I told him how we arrived at the opium compound on the evening of the third day, how we deployed around the camp in three groups, and how the Major, José, and I listened in on the drug deal. He perked up when I said that I had witnessed the drug deal, and he asked several questions about the Air America people who dealt with the opium growers. He took copious notes while I spoke and was very interested in what the CIA agents said, but he never revealed anything about his own thoughts. Periodically he would look up from his yellow legal pad and say, "I see," but that was his pat response to everything I said.

It was close to 2:00am when I finished my account. "Is there anything else I should know?" Mr. Jason inquired.

"Yes," I said. "During the mission, when we were watching the deal go down, the Major kept saying, "We thought this was going on." He said that several times, and he seemed to recognize the black guy who did the deal. He said, "This is something we have to get back. This is so important." He said what we were doing was of the "utmost" importance because it exposed the link between our government and the opium growers. And he emphasized that these government guys were with the CIA."

Mr. Jason looked at me quizzically. He turned off the tape recorder.

"I'm sure he said that to me, sir. I'm sure that was the object of the mission—to let you know that the CIA is doing drug deals with the enemy."

Mr. Jason's hands were folded on the desk in front of him. He wasn't taking notes anymore and that made me nervous. "Please go on," he said.

"While we were surveiling the opium compound, I kept thinking: "Here are government agents doing this, but the government says it's down on drugs. There's a dichotomy here because the opium becomes heroin and the heroin gets sold in America!"

Mr. Jason stared at me, but before he could say, "I see," I blurted out the question I had been longing to ask him. "So maybe you can tell me, sir, why is the CIA doing this? Is it just a few rotten apples?"

I had gotten a little excited, but he didn't seem to be offended. Putting the tape recorder and legal pad in his briefcase, he said: "What I can tell you is this: the CIA is gunning for you, as you know. You're in grave danger and we've got to get you out of the country as fast as possible."

He locked his attaché case, and then asked one of the security people in the hall to summon the lieutenant colonel. Then he shut the door and addressed me one last time.

"The Major and I, and everyone who put the mission together, are totally against what the CIA is doing. Now maybe you thought they were clean, and maybe it's hard for you to accept the fact that they're dirtier than most. But," and here his paternal voice was coldly indifferent, "the Agency has its own way of getting things done."

With that gratuitous remark, my heart sank. Mr. Jason had been patronizing me all along. Knowing the incident would be suppressed at the highest levels of government, in the name of national security, I said, mockingly, "I see." At that stage of the game I simply could not bring myself to admit that I had been defeated. To do so would have diminished the sacrifices of my comrades. But inside I knew that the mission had been a complete and utter waste. And that feeling has made all the difference.

Epilogue

Mr. Jason left with the film, as well as his audiotapes and handwritten notes of my account of what had transpired, and that same night I was flown to Tan Son Nhut and put on the next transport plane bound for the United States. We flew via Hawaii to Travis Air Force Base in California, where I was given a complete physical examination and a series of shots. During the two or three days I was at Travis, recuperating and calming down, I was quartered in a high security area under the constant protection of a Blue Beret security team. Though my role in the investigation had officially ended, the Air Force and Mr. Jason suspected that CIA agents, disguised as military officers, might try to infiltrate the base and assassinate me, as a reprisal.

Obviously that never happened.

Less than two weeks after I was initially approached about the mission, I returned to Cannon Air Force Base, happy to be alive. The gung-ho base Security Chief and Mr. Hammer debriefed me on the day I arrived, and when they were finished questioning me, I expressed my concern that the CIA would track me down at my job.

Their response was to smile and say, rather smugly, "Don't worry. You're covered."

"How's that?" I inquired.

"Two things," they said. First, the CIA wanted the film, not me; and second, I was never in Laos.

"What do you mean?"

"There were never any orders. The mission never happened. Not officially. So you're perfectly safe, as long as you don't mention it. Get the picture?"

Suddenly I did understand. The joke was on me.

"What you're saying is that the TDY orders were fake...that no written orders ever existed."

"On the contrary," they said. "The record shows you were in the Philippines. Officially you were never in Laos. What's more, for your protection as well as ours, if you say you were in Laos, we'll deny it ever happened."

The older men gave me back my military ID, social security card, and driver's license, and then they handed me twenty-five hundred dollars in cash. They added that I had done a good job, but I would not be decorated.

So I went back to work at the Public Information office where I resumed my normal duties and normal way of life, and put the episode behind me. I watched with resignation the escalation of the fighting in Southeast Asia, and the concurrent expansion of the anti-war movement at home. And as more and more reports surfaced about rising drug addiction among America's increasingly demoralized Armed Forces, the TDY mission seemed more pointless than ever.

The CIA had proven itself invincible.

*   *   *

Two years passed in the blink of an eye and in early 1969 I was approached again by the base Security Chief, this time without the knowledge of the Personnel Director or the base commander, and asked to take part in a secret photo-surveillance investigation that was being conducted into the activities of the base Supply Officer by the Tactical Air Command, the Air Force's Inspector General, and the National Security Agency.

The assignment was easy enough. The Supply Officer, a light colonel aptly named Wolf, was selling CAR-15s (the Air Force's version of the M-16) and other military items to right-wing civilians in the neighboring community, on what the investigators called "the American black market." NSA got involved because nuclear weapons were stored on base and there was some fear that Colonel Wolf might be passing along some of them, too, perhaps to agents of a foreign government.

To make a long story short we caught Wolf red-handed exchanging weapons for cash, and he wound up getting twenty years at Fort Leavenworth. But when the base commander found out—and this is a vast understatement—he became very upset. There was a rumor circulating around base that he was getting a percentage of the profits, and my part in the investigation put me right on the top of his hit-list. Certain NCOs in the base commander's office dropped some not so subtle hints that, if I valued my life, I should leave town by sundown. It was one of those extraordinary cases where going to Vietnam was safer than staying in the United States; and so with the help of my friends in Personnel, I applied for and was granted the first available overseas assignment.

In April 1969 I returned to Vietnam as part of a Top Secret Air Force operation called Operation Palace Dog, aka Project 404. Everyone assigned to Palace Dog fell under the operational control of MACV headquarters; we wore the red and yellow MACV shoulder patch with the sword, and were quartered at the heavily fortified MACV annex on Dong Khanh Street in Cholon, the predominantly Taiwanese Chinese section of Saigon. It was there that I learned, firsthand, as only an insider can, the ludicrous realities of the Vietnam War.

My job, ostensibly, was teaching the English language to South Vietnamese Air Force officers, all of who were exceptionally fast learners. The course lasted twenty-four weeks, after which the Vietnamese officers—all of whom invariably graduated—were shipped with their families (if they could afford to bring them along) to the United States for advanced training in the operation of jet aircraft and helicopters. Upon arriving in America, however, the Vietnamese officers inexplicably became incapable of further educational advancement and inevitably flunked out of the four month long training course, some after as many as three tries.

Having proven themselves unworthy of returning to South Vietnam to carry on the Holy Crusade against the Communists, they had no choice but to hang their heads in shame and remain with their families permanently, and safely, in America.

As the French say, "Vive la bagatelle!"

Just for the record, Palace Dog was essentially a gigantic red herring: or, as they say in the spy business, a "deep cover" for five or six CIA officers who posed as civilian instructors at the school. Outfitted with a plausible excuse for roaming the underworld of Saigon, the spooks were rarely in school. When they were, they distinguished themselves by acting arrogantly, giving orders to everyone, and taking advice from none.

They were typical CIA: totally undisciplined and overly impressed with themselves to the point of being deluded. Indeed, despite their omnipotence, none of them knew anything about my previous run-in with the Agency. Or so I thought.

The rest of us at the language school were US Air Force airmen acting under the direction of a US Army Special Forces Sergeant Major who had been living in South Vietnam for over six years, and had made a small fortune on the black market. The Sergeant Major's primary occupation was selling highly refined sand (gathered on the beaches near 5th Special Forces headquarters at Nha Trang) to Japanese engineers who processed the sand into ceramic for computer chips. As the owner of the ship that transported the sand, our Sergeant Major had amassed a considerable amount of gold bullion that he kept stashed in his beautiful villa. Like many of his fellow war profiteers, he remained in the Far East after the war, living the life of an exiled king.

Just to give you an idea of the type of man he was, I'll tell you a quick story about our Sergeant Major. Muscular, handsome, and in his early thirties, he was a brutal man with a charismatic personality. His body was covered with scars, the price for having fought all over the world, including Africa and Israel in 1967.

One night he and I were drinking in a bar in Cholon. We were standing at the bar talking, and behind us, his pretty Vietnamese wife was flirting with a South Vietnamese army officer. They were seated at a booth, and some heavy petting was going on, and what happened next was incredible but true.

The Sergeant Major walked over to the booth and assumed a martial arts stance, with his feet splayed, his left arm bent horizontally in front of his chest, and his right elbow tucked in at his hip. His right forearm was level with the floor and the fingers of his right hand were pointing straight at the Vietnamese officer's throat. He waited until the man realized he was standing there; then he yelled and his right hand shot forward, ripping out the ARVN officer's windpipe, killing him instantly. Blood gushed onto the table as the Sergeant Major disdainfully slapped a handful of flesh and veins in front of his horrified wife. With his right hand he pinned her against the back of the booth, then he pressed his right thumb through her delicate chest, directly into her heart, killing her instantly too.

Showing no remorse he returned to the bar, wiped his hands on a cloth, and ordered a round of drinks for the entire bar. The Filipino band played on.

That's exactly how it was in Saigon; no one gave a damn. If you weren't there you just can't comprehend how cheap life was. For a hundred dollars you could have anyone killed. It happened all the time. There was no escaping it. Which explains why everyone there was stoned on something. Within minutes of arriving at the MACV annex I was offered all kinds of drugs. And those who weren't getting stoned were getting drunk. Believe me, it was a huge lunatic asylum. And like I said, no one cared.

Money was the name of the game and I learned how to play the game well. I taught four hours a day, five days a week, and that's all. The rest of the time was mine, and in the afternoons the Vietnamese Air Force and Army officers would pay me as much as two hundred dollars a session to go to their homes and give private English language instruction to their families. It was a gold mine, and once the money started pouring in from my extracurricular tutoring, I moved out of the MACV annex into a hotel on Trung Huang Dao Street. My Vietnamese lover was living with me, I was making about three thousand dollars a month on the side, and I was doubling those earnings on the black market by changing military script and money, and by selling all sorts of commodities, from liquor and cigarettes to major appliances and marijuana.

Ironies abounded in Saigon and giving credit where credit is due, I must admit that the person who taught me how to thrive off the economy was one of the CIA instructors at the Palace Dog language school. This particular CIA officer was a black man who wore more gold rings, gold bracelets, and gold necklaces than Mr. T. (Remember him?) His contacts in the administrative offices at MACV would give him eighteen hours advance notice before the military cashed in its outstanding script, and on one occasion he came back to my apartment with a quarter of a million dollars worth of it. As unbelievable as it may sound, his share of the take was a cool fifty percent.

On another occasion he said, "I bet you a night with a woman that I can make ten thousand dollars today, wheeling and dealing." And he did it too, just for fun.

*   *   *

Toward the end of my tour in Vietnam, a member of my lover's family was placed on the Phoenix blacklist. The CIA's Phoenix Program was designed to neutralize Communists and Communist sympathizers, and anyone unfortunate enough to find himself on the Phoenix blacklist was subject to "administrative detention" in an interrogation center for as long as two years. In order to get my lover's name off the blacklist, I had to raise a lot of money fast. The black CIA agent from the Palace Dog language school knew it, and made a rather unorthodox proposal that I'll tell you about later on. In the meantime, I'll tell you about an event that changed my way of thinking.

The Palace Dog facility was located on Dong Khanh Street, the main drag between Saigon and Cholon. It was a four-story steel and concrete building with very tight security. The ground level was ringed with barbed wire, you needed a pass to get inside, and the roof had machine gun emplacements on all four corners. But the building was a symbol of the American presence and on 7 August 1969, the school was blown up by a car bomb.

I'll never forget that day. I was in the midst of teaching a class when we heard a commotion outside; people were yelling and there was gunfire. I looked out the window and saw that our guards were trying to stave off a Viet Cong attack, so I told the Vietnamese officers to get down and take cover under their desks. Just then bullets started exploding through the windows and the walls. Next there was a flash of light, then a tremendous explosion; shards of glass and pieces of shrapnel flew through the classroom cutting everyone including me. Some people in the building were killed, others badly wounded, but no one in my class suffered serious injury because I had had the common sense to tell them to duck down under their desks. And for that reason I was awarded the Vietnamese equivalent of the Medal of Honor.

My credits piled up fast as a result, but more importantly the car bombing made me realize that I was just as likely to get killed in downtown Saigon as any place else in South Vietnam. Coupled with everything else that had happened, the attack on the Palace Dog facility instilled in me a "fuck-it-all" attitude. I started thinking, "Why not move around the countryside for awhile and see how the Vietnamese live in their villages?" And that's what I did. In October 1969 I volunteered for an additional six months in-country. By doing so I was committed to seeing some action, but by volunteering for the extra six months in-country I would be discharged from the Air Force immediately upon returning to the United States, rather than spending another year in uniform—and that made the risk worthwhile.

The Air Force officer I reported to, Captain Seale, arranged for me to get a job as the liaison between the commanding officers of a Vietnamese Ranger outfit and their six Special Forces advisors. I was, in essence, a glorified translator-interpreter.

The Ranger compound was stationed in Tay Ninh, and our duty consisted primarily of conducting Search and Destroy missions, usually lasting three or four days, "over the fence" in Cambodia. The Vietnamese Rangers were absolutely the best at this type of work. They performed well in the field and had respect for enlisted men like me who did not affect a superior attitude or give them stupid orders. They knew my common-law wife was pregnant and that I had every intention of taking her back to the United States with me. So I developed a rapport with them. And despite the fact that "Search and Destroy" was a euphemism for "kill everyone in sight," I can honestly say that the Rangers believed their marauding was ensuring the freedom of their countrymen.

Anyway, with each successive Search and Destroy Mission into Cambodia, the size and scope of our operations grew. What began as platoon-sized incursions, with me as the only translator, soon grew to include three hundred Rangers, then five. Our battalion-sized outfit was broken into three companies, each accompanied by an American translator. As the Team Leader of the translators I accompanied our commanding officers and stayed at their side, but I still went on missions.

Our last mission was a major operation into an area that was heavily infested with Viet Cong guerrillas and their sympathizers. The village we destroyed was heavily supplied and we were in the process of stacking the rice and ammunition—with the intention of blowing them up—when we were counter-attacked by a unit of NVA regulars reinforced by VC. And they did to us what we had been doing to them.

We were surrounded in the village, so our Special Forces advisors deployed the Rangers in a perimeter defense. But we had been taken by surprise and half of the Rangers were killed in the first ten minutes as they tried to move into position. The North Vietnamese knew exactly where and when to hit us, and to this day I'm convinced that we were betrayed by an informer in our ranks.

Mortars, small artillery, and machine gun fire poured in on us while the Special Forces advisors organized a second line of defense. After the shelling came the ground assault, and it was bad. It was the heaviest combat I had ever experienced. A mortar landed near our position killing two of the other translators instantly. Pieces of their bodies were scattered everywhere. Dead and wounded men were all around me. There was screaming and yelling and crying.

I had a slight concussion from the mortar blast and my vision was fuzzy, but I could see a squad of sappers advancing on our position through the smoke and the carnage. The sappers had satchel charges and I knew I had to do something, so I killed them. I blew them away with my M-16. The most bizarre things happen in combat and quite by chance one of my bullets hit their satchel charge and sent them sky high—and that, surprisingly, ended the assault, although the explosion was so close it knocked me unconscious. I don't even recall the choppers coming in, but the next thing I knew I was back in the field hospital in Tay Ninh.

That was a week or two before Christmas, 1969, and it was several days before my hearing and vision returned to normal. But as soon as I recovered I swore off cross-border operations forever. No more marauding for me.

Now don't get me wrong. America should not have been in Vietnam in the first place, but some of us found ourselves there, in much the same way I had been tricked into the TDY mission. And once we were there we had to protect ourselves if we wanted to survive. And sometimes a good offense is the best defense.

That's the point I'm trying to make in this Epilogue.

What we had to do to survive doesn't bother me. What bothers me is the knowledge that our leaders conspired with Hanoi, Peking, and Moscow not to expand the war. In effect, they collaborated with the enemy and should be shot as traitors, just like the CIA agents who were running drugs in Laos.

It was the corporate politicians and generals who lost the war, not the press or the war protestors, and that's a hard pill for the true believers to swallow.

Please allow me to elaborate.

Following the obliteration of my Ranger outfit, Captain Seale had me relieved of further combat duty and I was transferred back to the language school. My life rebounded and once again good fortune came my way. Pleased by my performance and successful adjustment to Vietnamese culture, my superiors at MACV assigned me on a part time basis to teach field grade Vietnamese Army and Air Force officers at a beautiful French villa on Tu Do Street, not far from the Majestic Hotel. My common-law wife, Lu Dui, had given birth to our first child, Phuong. The South Vietnamese officers were inviting me to official and social gatherings, and at these in-crowd parties I was introduced to people from the US Embassy.

One of the people I met, a Special Assistant to the Ambassador, befriended me when we discovered that we came from the same town in New York. We often met for meals at the Caravelle and the Tempura House, but we argued a lot too. Like most State Department officials, Sam had a patronizing attitude toward our allies; he staunchly maintained that East was East and West was West and never the twain would meet. Sam could never forget that America's long term interests came first.

Our differences were entirely academic, however, and we enjoyed one another's company tremendously. Within a very short period of time we became close friends. It may even have been more than that. At times it was like father and son.

In any event, time moved at an accelerated pace in Saigon, and soon my tour was drawing to its inevitable conclusion. So I began to make preparations to bring Lu Dui and Phuong back home with me. However, when the Air Force ran a security check on my wife, they found that she had a relative in the Viet Cong Infrastructure.

As the secret police already knew, everyone in South Vietnam had relatives in the Viet Cong Infrastructure. But for that or some other unstated reason the US Air Force refused to allow her to travel with me to the United States.

In desperation I turned to Sam for help, and he told me the solution to my problem was, as usual, money. The price for bribing the proper Phoenix officials, in order to have Lu's name moved from the blacklist, was twenty thousand dollars.

The possibilities of raising that much money, in the short amount of time I had left in-country, were slim. So Sam approached the CIA and the CIA offered to hire me as a contract employee. The deal was that I would remain in Saigon as a civilian and continue working as a language instructor for ranking Vietnamese officers and their families. The CIA, through the black agent at the Palace Dog language school, offered me fifteen grand a year, plus room, board and expenses, and they reminded me that I knew how to turn the base pay into considerably more on the black market.

But I didn't like the idea of being blackmailed into joining the CIA. Some contracts you can never get out of, and I suspected it was an attempt to guarantee my silence about the TDY mission, so I said, "No thanks."

There were still other opportunities available, and next Sam introduced me to representatives from Texaco and Mobile Oil. They were drilling for oil and during dinner at the Continental Hotel, they talked about the concessions they had acquired in South Vietnam and Cambodia, and how business was booming. And it was then that I realized we were fighting the war for them. I leaned across the table and said, "We're here to protect the mineral rights, right?"

They didn't like hearing it put that way and neither did Sam, and that ruined my chances of working for any of his business contacts—which were everywhere. Walk down any street in Saigon and you would see signs for Mekong Ford and Bank of America. There were Shell stations (which were never attacked) sitting beside false leg factories and companies that mass-produced coffins. The US Army was guarding the Michelin rubber plantation and the Nong Son coal mine. By the end of 1970, Union Oil, with the help of the Nixon Administration, had bought the concession to all on-shore oil in Cambodia, and was gobbling up the off-shore concessions too.

You might not know this, but not one American oil truck was ever sabotaged in Vietnam. Do you realize how much protection money the oil companies had to pay the Viet Cong? Do you have any idea what the VC used that money for?

They called it "Vietnamization" but it was really "Americanization." There was just too much money to be made.

Meanwhile I was running out of time, and I was confused too. The Air Force, which had treated me well, would not let me leave with my wife, probably at the insistence of the CIA. My only remaining option was to go to work for the CIA, which I had once considered my mortal enemy. And just when I needed money most I had a pang of conscience and realized that profiteering—the type of profiteering I had been fully engaged in—was the root cause of the Vietnam War.

I could not bring myself to work for the CIA, so I turned against the war and joined Saigon's underground chapter of the VVAW, thinking and hoping they might help.

The people who formed the VVAW in Saigon did so as a way of exposing all the massive cover-ups that were occurring: the My Lai massacre, the Phoenix Program, the Green Beret murder case, drug smuggling, and military operations inside Laos and Cambodia. All the news the *New York Times* had decided was not fit to print.

Some VVAW members were working inside MACV headquarters and saw the news before it was censored. They were on the information front lines and they had connections. But the VVAW in Saigon was very loosely organized. There were no membership cards and no newsletter. Members were leaking information, yes, but no one was speaking out loud. That would have been crazy. Suicidal.

To make a long story short, there was nothing the VVAW could do, and when time ran out, I got on the plane and went home alone.

It wasn't easy and I had every intention of going back for Lu Dui and Phuong. But the longer I stayed away, the harder it got. And finally I just gave up.

The guilt I feel about that has never subsided.

*   *   *

Please let me conclude my story about CIA drug smuggling, and my reasons for turning against the Vietnam War, by acknowledging that I was as responsible for the tragedy as anyone else, for all the reasons cited above. As I said at the beginning of Chapter Thirteen, the only difference between a true believer and me, is that I have done more than merely believe. I have tried to acknowledge and analyze my own responsibility as well.

For what it's worth.

Afterword

My eyes collide head on with stuffed graveyards
False gods, I scuff
At pettiness that plays so rough
Walk upside-down inside handcuffs
Kick my legs to crash it off
Say okay, I have had enough
What else can you show me?

        "It's Alright Ma (I'm Only Bleeding)"
        Bob Dylan
        Copyright 1965, 1966 M Witmark & Sons

Made in the USA
Middletown, DE
17 July 2021